P9-CDJ-093

EXIT, PURSUED BY A BEAR

E. K. JOHNSTON

WITHDRAWN

DUTTON BOOKS

Fitchburg Public Library
5530 Lacy Road
Fitchburg, WI 53711

Dutton Books
An imprint of Penguin Random House LLC
375 Hudson Street
New York, NY 10014

Copyright © 2016 by E. K. Johnston.

Penguin supports copyright. Copyright fuels creativity, encourages diverse voices, promotes free speech, and creates a vibrant culture. Thank you for buying an authorized edition of this book and for complying with copyright laws by not reproducing, scanning, or distributing any part of it in any form without permission. You are supporting writers and allowing Penguin to continue to publish books for every reader.

This is a work of fiction. Names, characters, places, and incidents either are the product of the author's imagination or are used fictitiously, and any resemblance to actual persons, living or dead, businesses, companies, events, or locales is entirely coincidental.

Library of Congress Cataloging-in-Publication Data

Names: Johnston, E. K., author.
Title: Exit, pursued by a bear / by E.K. Johnston.
Description: New York, NY : Dutton BOOKS, an imprint of Penguin Random House LLC, [2016]
Summary: At cheerleading camp, Hermione is drugged and raped, but she is not sure whether it was one of her teammates or a boy on another team—and in the aftermath she has to deal with the rumors in her small Ontario town, the often awkward reaction of her classmates, the rejection of her boyfriend, the discovery that her best friend, Polly, is gay, and above all the need to remember what happened so that the guilty boy can be brought to justice.
Identifiers: LCCN 2015020645 | ISBN 9781101994580 (hardcover)
Subjects: LCSH: Rape victims—Juvenile fiction. | Psychic trauma—Juvenile fiction. | Cheerleading—Juvenile fiction. | High schools—Juvenile fiction. | Social isolation—Juvenile fiction. | Best friends—Juvenile fiction. | Friendship—Juvenile fiction. | Ontario—Juvenile fiction. | CYAC: Rape—Fiction. | Emotional problems—Fiction. | Cheerleading—Fiction. | High schools—Fiction. | Schools—Fiction. | Social isolation—Fiction. | Best friends—Fiction. | Friendship—Fiction. | Ontario—Fiction. | Canada—Fiction.
Classification: LCC PZ7.J64052 Ex 2016 | DDC [Fic]—dc23 LC record available at lccn.loc.gov/2015020645

Printed in the United States of America
ISBN 978-1-101-99458-0

10 9 8 7 6 5 4 3 2 1

Design by Kristin Logsdon
Text set in Sabon

To Andrew,
Because: [reasons].

"I have a secret.
A dark, furry secret with big teeth.
Less a secret, really—more a bear."
—Oglaf

"I never saw a vessel of like sorrow,
so fill'd and so becoming."
—*The Winter's Tale*

I START RUNNING AFTER SCHOOL. Usually I get enough of a workout between practice and gym class that I don't do extra, but this week I feel like I might explode if I stop moving. So I run. I run up and down the streets of Palermo, looking at the houses and coloured leaves on the trees and trying to hold on to the feeling that my body is my own and limitless. I run on the country roads, the gravel crunching under my feet—until the smell of pine makes me feel sick and I fly back to the safety of concrete sidewalks. I run and run, and when I finally fall asleep at night, I am tired enough that I don't remember my dreams.

One night, I pass the church my father and I attend whenever we're both home on Sunday morning (so . . . about once a month, in a good month). I've passed the church every other night this week, but tonight the light in the office is on. Once upon a time, churches were always open, a sanctuary if you needed them. But the world changes, I guess. I haven't given a single thought to the church since it happened, but when I see the light on, my feet slow down of their own accord, and I am knocking on the door before I know it. My fist sounds heavy against the wood. I am already having second thoughts, but it would be rude to run away. Just when I think maybe the light was left on accidentally, the door opens, and there is the minister, dressed in normal clothes, and looking a bit confused. When he sees me, his eyes widen for a moment before he makes his face neutral.

"Hello, Hermione," he says. I wonder if he remembers my name because he's good at his job or because I've been on the news. He doesn't ask me if I'm okay. Instead he waves me in, and shuts the door. Maybe it's because I'm in a church. Maybe it's because this is the man who baptized me. But I'm not afraid.

"Hello, Reverend Rob," I say, and the door latch echoes in the hallway. "I'm not interrupting anything, am I?"

"No, no. Just practicing for Sunday. All this time, and I still get a bit of stage fright leading up to a sermon."

I follow Rob back into his office, which is warmly lit and full of old books. He waves me into one of the seats. I have just realized what it is I want to say, what I want to ask him.

"Would you like water or tea?" he asks. "That's all I have on hand."

"I'm fine, thank you," I say, feeling profoundly awkward. I keep finding new ways to do that. "I don't come here very often."

"That's okay." He's sitting comfortably in his chair. People are never comfortable around me anymore. "I know how life goes. Schedules and the Church don't always get along, so I do my best to operate an open door policy."

"Right," I say. "I have two favours to ask. One's a bit presumptuous. The other is . . . also presumptuous."

"Please. Feel free to ask."

"Thank you." I pause for a moment to gather my thoughts. I think of the looks I've been getting at the grocery store, and take a deep breath. "Please don't ask people to pray for me."

PART 1

And summer's lease hath all too short a date.

CHAPTER 1

I SWEAR TO GOD, LEO, if you throw one more sock, I am going to throw you in the lake myself!" I shout, knees sticking to the vinyl as I turn to face the back of the bus. The boys had claimed the back when we boarded, and since it smelled weird (well, more weird), we were happy to let them have it. I hadn't expected a constant barrage of hosiery, though.

"Like you could, Winters," he shouts back. The other boys hoot in laughter.

"I may be small," I reply, "but I'm crafty."

"Don't I know it," Leo leers, and the hooting devolves into outright catcalls.

I fire back with a wadded sock, barely missing Leo but managing to nail Clarence, who looks properly chastened. I glare at the rest and then turn sharply to face the front, but by the time I'm in my seat again, I'm smiling. The other girls lean in towards me, ribboned braids dropping over shoulders like the least-threatening snake pile in the world. Of course, that's what the snakes probably want you to think.

I can feel the pavement change beneath the bus. Just one step above gravel. We're close now.

"Seriously, Hermione," Polly whispers just loud enough for the other girls to hear. My co-captain and best friend feels it too. "We're putting Leo's ass in the lake this year."

"Please. We've got to come up with something better than that!"

"Totally," squeals Astrid, who is fifteen and will agree to anything Polly and I say. The power is dangerous, or it could be. It's definitely fun.

"This is going to be the best cheer camp ever," says another new girl as she leans over the back of the bench. She's still so short I bet her knees are lifting off her seat as she tries to get closer to me and Polly. I can't remember her name. That's inexcusable. I have to be better.

"Girls," I say, like I'm telling them the secrets of the universe, "this *is* going to be the best cheer *year* ever."

"Go Bears!" shouts Polly, flinging her perfectly manicured hands in the air and shaking pom-poms she doesn't have. The boys are stomping along in back. Even the bus driver is in her spell, and I catch him looking back and smiling in his mirror. I'm the only one who knows her well enough to know that she is being excruciatingly sarcastic. That is Polly's superpower. She's a cheerleader for want of another choice, and while she looks like the perfect model, underneath the plastic veneer is a capacity for scorn and contempt I'm glad is on my side. Whatever the odds, if Polly is cheering for you, you are a force to be reckoned with.

As always, Polly's carefully timed and cultivated enthusiasm is contagious, and as we planned, when the bus rolls under the huge wooden WELCOME TO CAMP MANITOUWABING sign, the windows are down and the whole lot of us are singing about how much we love our school and how proud we are to be the Fighting Golden Bears. Polly might think it's ridiculous—and she's probably right—but I don't care. We're a team, from the newest recruits trying desperately to fit in, to my boyfriend, who has still not stopped throwing laundry at my head. We're a team and we're entering my last-ever camp as the loudest and proudest one here. I wouldn't have it another way.

The bus pulls to a stop, tires crunching on the unpaved drive, and we stay in our seats as a minivan pulls up beside us. Coach Caledon gets out. She stretches for a moment, and her perfectly straight jet-black hair nearly touches the ground. She's around forty but her face is smooth, with skin a colour we'd all kill for. She still has an athlete's body—thin, muscular, and supremely coordinated—but I know she tore an ACL in university, and long car rides are hard on her. When she's loose enough to walk without a perceptible limp, she heads for the office. Meanwhile, her daughter flies out of the passenger seat and a moment later vaults the bus's steps in one very impressive leap when the driver opens the door for her.

"Hey, everybody!" she calls out. Florry's only ten, but we all love her to death. I'm a little sad I won't be around when she starts her high-school cheering career. "Mom's gone to get registration and cabin assignments. She wants you all to sit tight until she gets here."

It says something about the power of Alexandra Caledon that her directions can be delivered by a ten-year-old and lose none of their effectiveness. We stay in our seats, as ordered, until Caledon finally climbs the stairs.

"Okay, ladies and gentlemen, as you've noticed, we have arrived at Camp Manitouwabing," she says. She makes this speech every year. It's reassuring and it reminds me once again of how excited I am. "Hermione, Polly, Leo and Tig all know the drill, so if you have questions, go to them before you come to me. I'm handing out your cabin assignments now." She pauses as she holds several sheets of paper where we can see them. "You will note that some cabins are for boys and some cabins are for girls—"

"Let's keep it that way!" chant those of us who know. I notice Leo and Tig snickering.

"Indeed." Caledon says it lightly, but the implied threat is more than enough to make us pay attention. As she continues, she hands a sheet to me. "Also, should you seriously injure yourself, it is an hour to Parry Sound and an airlift to Toronto. And a lot of paperwork for me. So don't do it. There will be a bell in half an hour for the intro presentation. Please be prompt. Until then, you can settle in."

I look down at my list. Since Polly and I are holding separate lists, I'm thinking this year is a mixer. Some years, the camp puts all the same school into the same cabin, and some years they mix it up. I'd curse if Caledon wasn't right there. It's hard to plot and stay up to all hours with Polly when she's in another cabin. Polly looks insufferably perky. She must be super annoyed too.

"Astrid, Jenny, Alexis, Carmen and Mallory," I call out. "You're with me."

"Which means I get Chelsea, Brenda, Karen and both Sarahs," Polly continues, never missing a beat. I can't help but smile.

Both Sarahs sigh. You'd think the camp admin people would have taken the opportunity to split them up.

"Don't worry, ladies!" says Tig, who is holding his own list. "Hopefully by the end of camp, you'll have nicknames and we'll be able to tell you apart."

"Yeah," says Astrid, showing more personality than I'd expected this early. "Awesome nicknames like Tig."

Tig, who is actually called Andrew, turns bright red. He feels the name is undignified, though he has never been able to shake it. It galls him a little, I think, that Leo's camp nickname never stuck.

We file off the bus. The air feels cooler—and smells better—than it did on the unairconditioned bus. And there is that unmistakable mix of summer heat and cool pine. Mallory, who's also here for the last time, launches a quick front handspring. A captain has to keep up appearances or I'd join her. I've been waiting a long time for this.

At the back of the bus, Tig and Dion—who've somehow lost their shirts—are ready to pass us our bags. The boys have packed one duffel apiece, which is infuriating. Given the choice,

I'm a light packer, but two weeks at cheer camp means two weeks of looking absolutely perfect every time I leave the cabin. It's the one thing about cheerleading I really hate. I love flying and shouting and gymnastics, but I really don't like spending twenty minutes on my makeup before sunrise and coming up with fourteen different ways to do my hair.

The boys extricate themselves pretty quickly, leaving us behind to sort out who belongs to which makeup case. Per a team tradition so old even I don't know when it started, we all have matching cases. We'd tied ribbons on the handles when we packed, but it turns out that before the boys started their hosiery skirmish, they'd done some fairly serious ribbon switching. I amend my earlier plan to drown Leo to include all six of them.

Fifteen minutes later, I lead my five girls off to the cabin we'll be sharing with, if my memory of school colours is correct, St. Ignatius from Mississauga. Their purple and orange will be at odds with our gold, black, and white, and the photos won't be as nice as last year's, but there's not a lot I can do about that. I just hope they haven't done something annoying like claimed all the bottom bunks.

Polly is beside me, her girls ranged out behind her like ducklings. She's bound for a cabin flying green and white, which means it's either the Kincardine Knights or that private school from Thunder Bay whose mascot I can never recall because it's conceptual.

"Buck up," she says, reading my expression. "It's cheer camp. What's the worst that could happen?"

I've been waiting for this moment, or one like it, my whole life. I can handle getting stuck with the top bunk. I square my shoulders and heft my backpack, indicating to Polly that I don't find her question worth the air to answer, and start walking.

Polly laughs, and turns towards her cabin.

The rickety front porch of our new home is in the shade, which means it will be a bit cooler. Of course, that also means there will be about a million mosquitoes, but if there's new netting it's an even trade in my experience. But I'm getting ahead of myself.

Mallory passes me the school colours. I take a deep breath, and then scale the railing to tie them on next to the St. Ignatius colours. They clash as horribly as expected, but once the wind picks up, I don't really care. I look down at my team, all of whom are bouncing like coiled springs, just like I always did when my captain hung the colours. I can feel their excitement. It really is going to be the best year ever.

"Girls," I yell, suddenly unbearably aware that I will never say these words again, "let's do this thing!"

CHAPTER 2

CAMP MANITOUWABING IS ONE OF those summer camps that looks like it has been around forever. 'Wabing used to be a Kiwanis camp, and before that it was an RAF training camp, and before that it was a retreat for the king of Norway. Or something. But whatever it used to be, what remains are twenty campers' cabins with peeling brown clapboard sides and sloping green roofs, six slightly better maintained staff cabins, a wide green field painted with football lines, an aging dock, and a sprawling dining hall.

"Hi!" says the girl I can only assume is the St. Ignatius captain when I open the door to the cabin. I've probably seen her before, but while my brain is good at colours, faces start to blur after a while. She extends one hand, the nails painted purple and orange. "I'm Amy."

I introduce myself as the rest of the girls trickle in behind me. Her hands full, Mallory can't catch the screen door as it swings back. All of us who have been here before brace ourselves for the loud crash as it closes, but Amy catches it before it does. She shuts the door silently and smiles as she does it.

I look around and see that they've chosen to occupy one side of the cabin. I couldn't care less what side of this cabin we get. I know this one's roof doesn't leak unlike the one we stayed in my first year. Polly and I ended up sleeping together in the bottom bunk. "Good catch," I say, smiling at the memory—and at Amy's quick work with the screen door.

Mallory and I pair up, and without a word she gives me captain's choice of the bottom bunk. We all start unpacking, which is mostly limited to putting suitcases under beds and unrolling sleeping bags, but the bell rings long before we're done.

"Don't worry too much," Mallory, who has nearly as many camps under her belt as I do, tells Astrid, who is perched on her bunk trying to straighten her sleeping bag as if her life depended on it. "We'll have some spare time to unpack later."

"Yeah," I say loudly, kicking my own still-rolled bag to the foot of the bunk. "And you really don't want to be late, trust me."

Amy nods knowingly from across the cabin, and marshals her teammates. She's got her own newbies to deal with, it seems. We head out together, mixing with one another cautiously, trading names and testing the waters. Everyone gathers on the field, and we sit through the intro with the late August sun beating down on us.

I've heard this intro several times, so my mind wanders while the staff is introduced. I remember the first time Polly and I were here, before we started grade nine. We'd worked hard to make the team. I was terrified of Caledon, even though I had been to her development camps since the summer I was first eligible for them. She'd been tough then, but it was even worse now. Polly and I both did as much as we could, but the pressure was intense and the odds were against us. It was very unusual for grade nines to make it through tryouts. Most of the rookies were going into grade ten. But Caledon is always scrupulously fair. She would tour the elementary schools at the end of June and invite people she thought had a shot to a special tryout with the existing team. They nearly always get cut, but Polly and I both scraped through.

I remember those moments of terror as the list was posted. Lindsay, the captain at the time, was standing beside the paper to congratulate or console, as required. I'm sure she meant to be reassuring, but instead it felt like we should expect the worst. What if I made it and Polly didn't? What if Polly made it and I didn't? I wanted to be on the team because I loved it. Polly was a little different. Palermo Heights is small, so our few sports teams aren't great—if you're being charitable. So as long as anyone can remember, if you wanted to be noticed and to win at something in Palermo Heights, you had to be a cheerleader, and Polly wanted to win more than any person I'd ever met. When I saw the list with both our names on it, I almost didn't believe it. It wasn't entirely real until we were both sitting on this field, with the sun on our French-braided hair, and our gold ribbons scratching against the skin on the backs of our necks.

Two months ago, it had been my duty to be the grade-twelve cheerleader waiting to console the disappointed would-be rookies and to balance that with welcoming the successful ones. Fortunately, I am very good at balance.

I tune back in just as the camp director talks about the swim test we all have to pass that afternoon if we want to go swimming at all during camp. I know from experience that the lake will be absolutely freezing but also that swimming is much faster than waiting for the shower after practice.

Leo catches my eye across the field and winks at me, and I get the feeling he's been watching me the whole time I was remembering. He does that a lot—stare at me, I mean. I guess that's a normal thing for a boyfriend to do, but I never seem to find myself staring back. Usually I just get the end of it, and feel like I've missed something. Leo seems to have the answers, and I'm not sure I know the question.

"And tonight, after the swimming and dinner," the director wraps up as she always does, "there will be a campfire down by the lake. Each captain will tell a story about their squad that is something the team is not proud of. This will be the story of a failure or shortcoming that your team has had to deal with. Your goal for the next two weeks will be to come together and solve those problems, both as a team, and as campers in general. Once again, welcome to Camp Manitouwabing. I hope you all have a great time, and I'll see you at the lake!"

There's some cheering at that—we are cheerleaders after

all—and then everyone drifts back to their cabins to change. There's going to be a huge lineup for the test regardless, so I don't hurry too much. Yes, I should probably set an example, but mostly I am not looking forward to another two hours under the sun. At least if I'm swimming I can take the ribbons out of my hair. Polly brushes my shoulder in the crowd, and I smile at her as she heads off towards her cabin.

We haven't told anyone this, not even Caledon, but this bonfire tonight is one of the reasons we wanted so badly to be co-captains this year. Every year, we've had to sit there and listen to the captain go on and on about how underprivileged our school is, and how hard we have to fight because we're small. The captains from the bigger schools typically moan about not getting any respect, about not being treated like real athletes. It's all ridiculously irrelevant. Palermo Heights graduates give the cheerleading program more money than we know what to do with (we are, for example, not paying anything out of pocket to attend this camp and we are the only team at the school with uniforms from this decade). We are the reason the Palermo newspaper has a sports section. If there was cellular service at camp, everybody back home would be following our Instagram accounts. Cheerleading at Palermo Heights is simply a different animal. So Polly and I have plans for this bonfire, plans that are bigger than the squad and the two weeks we'll spend at camp. It's entirely possible that our teammates won't like it, but every time I get nervous about it, Polly makes sure my spine stays firmly in place.

"I was really glad to see that you and Polly were made co-captains this year," Amy says, suddenly beside me. I can't make a habit of zoning out like this.

"We're excited too," I say. And it's the truth, but there's more to it than excitement. I think Amy knows it too.

"Sometimes co-captains just lead to a mess," Amy continues. I remember where I know her from now. St. Ignatius had co-captains last year, and it *was* a disaster. The two girls didn't agree on anything, and the whole team imploded. Amy was one of their fliers, and they dropped her at their final competition last season because they were so out of sync. She's going to be hungry this year, but at least her campfire story will be easy.

"Yeah," I say. "But Polly and I have been friends for a really long time, and we're ready to work together."

The truth is that Polly and I are almost ideal complements of each other. She is the aesthetically perfect one. She never has a hair out of place, and if she's done your hair, it will be perfect too. She's never met a face she couldn't do perfect makeup on, never met a tear she couldn't stitch up so it becomes invisible, and she does it all with a perfect white smile. I'm the choreographer. I can tell exactly how hard to push a new girl. I can convince the boys to stop goofing off and pay attention. I can corral eighteen hormonal teenagers, however momentarily, into a cohesive group capable of getting ordinary humans to fly. Polly will make sure you look perfect when you land, and I'm the one that will make sure someone is in the right place to catch you. Amy's not wrong: We're a great team. We ought to be. We're years in the making.

━━
━━

When Amy and I walk into the cabin, there are clothes everywhere as girls whose locker-room modesty faded long ago switch their tank tops and shorts for bathing suits. The newer girls try to look like they don't want to change inside their sleeping bags. Carmen winks at me. We've been doing this so long that we barely remember those days. There's an equal mix of overly sexy bikinis and practical one-pieces (though most of those are still in vibrant colours), and towels and sarongs in every shade imaginable.

"Mallory, are you set?" I shout out through the mass of people.

"Yeah," she says.

"Great. Take anyone who is ready with you. I have to find my shoes, and then I'll bring the rest." I rummage through my bag for my flip-flops as the crowd thins out around me. They're at the bottom, under my pajamas. As I throw my towel on my bed, I find a weird package in my luggage I know for sure I didn't pack. It's poorly wrapped and sealed with duct tape, so I know instantly that it's from Leo. I have to get my manicure scissors to unwrap it, and by then the cabin is mostly empty. I remind myself not to get frustrated, that the line will be long no matter what I do, but I don't like standing still when all my team members are gone ahead of me. Still, my curiosity is killing me. He must have put it in my bag when he and the other guys switched all the ribbons.

I cut the last of the tape, and the package all but falls apart in my hands. Immediately, I turn bright pink and shove the whole thing into my bag. Leo, in his esteemed wisdom, has given me a box of condoms.

Apparently I didn't make my plans for camp quite crystal clear. I am going to kill him.

I grab my shoes and head for the door. Jenny is standing there, clearly having waited for me, and for a moment I'm concerned that she saw the stupid present Leo gave me. She doesn't say anything, though, and her face is completely clear of suspicion or mockery.

"Ready?" she asks.

"Yes," I say. "Thanks for waiting."

"Anytime," she says brightly. And I do my best to forget about it.

CHAPTER 3

WE ALL PASS THE SWIM test, which is not a surprise. That's not the true test of the first day at Camp Manitouwabing. What really separates the weak from the strong is your ability to get into the dining hall.

To begin with, and I cannot stress this enough, order is of deadly importance. It's slightly more important at breakfast because cold eggs are vile, but even at dinner, it is crucial to be the first or second cabin to go in. Order used to be decided based on cabin inspections, which the girls invariably failed because it is impossible to keep that volume of makeup and hair accessories contained. Now the order is decided based on pre-meal cheering, to be improvised to whatever the theme of the day is. Volume is important, but so is enthusiasm and precision. I love

Polly. And Leo—though we're clearly still working out the details of our relationship—is my boyfriend. But when it comes to meals, I will gladly wipe the floor with both of them so that my cabin can eat first.

Amy smiles when I tell her as much, and leans in to bump against my shoulder like Polly would have done, were she not now our common enemy. I'm confident Amy's more loyal to her stomach than to St. Ignatius.

"The theme's 'beginning,' " says Mallory, breathing hard. I appreciate her initiative. She must have run ahead to check.

"Line 'em up," I say, and both Mallory and Amy move off to get the girls in order.

The cheering can't start until everyone has arrived and is standing in line with their cabins. That usually means you have about three minutes to plan. "Beginning" is a bit of a softball, to be honest. By the end of the week, the themes will be much more esoteric.

First order of business is to get a sense of the cabin's assets. My half of the cabin has three fliers and three bases.

"We're all fliers," says Amy apologetically, anticipating my question.

I sigh, but I'm not really surprised. Ignatius has a lot of guys on their team, so almost all their girls are fliers. We're going to have to win this one yelling.

"Okay, girls," I say, my best captain face firmly in place. "This is what we're going to do."

It's not the best plan, and it's a far cry from my best poetry,

17

but when the signal is given and we all start to chant in perfect unison, I know I've made the right call.

THE CHEER'S
THE THING
TO CATCH THE SPIRIT
WE BEGIN

The other cabins have tried to be more flashy, but since they only just met their cabin mates five hours ago, they're not particularly coordinated. We, on the other hand, are a well-oiled yelling machine, each repetition of the chant building on the one before it to create a pretty decent cadence. When the camp director waves us forward, Amy stops chanting and squeals, wrapping her arms around my neck. I can't help but return the gesture. There are a couple of impromptu cartwheels as we make our way inside. I lock eyes with Polly, who is supposed to be spotting a flier, and she makes a face at me. Astrid loops her arm through mine, and an Ignatius girl pats me on the back. We might not be a real team, but we're a team for now, and we've just won a hot dinner, so things are pretty good.

While we eat, the other teams come in behind us and get their food. You don't have to sit by cabin, so I save Polly a seat when it becomes apparent that my cabin is not going to let me break off and sit with anyone else. I eat as slowly as I can so I won't be completely done by the time she sits down, but Salisbury steak is gross enough hot, so I don't linger too long.

"I can't believe you won with a shout!" Polly says, slamming her tray down.

"Hey, there was a dance in there too!" I protest, but then smile as befits a gracious winner. "It'll never happen again."

"Damn straight," says Polly. "I'm going to kick your ass all week."

"You're in a cabin of fliers," I point out.

"We've got Brenda," she fires back. "Plus we've got my not-inconsequential intellect."

"True enough. Now eat, before it gets colder."

"Bite me."

"That's my job," says Leo, leaning in to kiss me on the cheek. I push him off. We talked about this before we got here, that camp was two weeks to work, to go out on top. We would not fool around. But Leo seems determined to be as annoying as possible. The condoms were clearly just his opening move.

When we started dating, everyone assured me that we were perfect for each other, but now I'm starting to wish I'd established better ground rules and enforced them from the start. He always looks at me like he has expectations that I never meet the way he wants, like right now.

"You didn't save me a seat."

"I'm unusually popular," I say, trying to play it down. It's just dinner. "It comes with being a cheerleader."

"You wound me, madam," he says extravagantly, one hand over his heart and his hair artfully falling over his forehead. Half of the girls at the table are staring at him, and the other half are working overtime not to. He is the perfect picture, and for a moment I forget that I'm mad at him.

"You all ready for the fire?" Tig says from his usual place at Leo's elbow. "Another year of the small, downtrodden country school."

"Something like that," says Polly. "But I'd hate to ruin the surprise, so go sit somewhere and leave us alone."

When the boys wander off and the girls turn to one another, I lean over to Polly.

"Do you think we should have mentioned it to Caledon?" I ask. "I mean, do you think she'll be mad?"

"Have you ever known our coach to be anything less than ferocious?" Polly counters. "She might not be thrilled, but I think she'll be proud of us, even if her teacher persona has to be reproving."

"I do so love it when you use big words," I swoon, affecting my best *Steel Magnolias* accent.

"Just don't chicken out on me," she says. "You're the one that's going to have to do all the talking."

I haven't forgotten. And I continue to not forget during the rapidly melting Jell-O we eat for dessert. By then, the sun is setting over the lake, and we head back to our cabins for sweatshirts we probably won't need and for bug spray we definitely will. By the time everyone makes it to the fire pit, it's well into dusk. That's my favourite time at camp. For the city kids, it might be the first time they've seen this many stars and the quietest moment they've ever known, but for me, it's coming into focus, coming home.

The fire pit is really a miniature stadium, set up to accommodate some two hundred people. The fire itself is on the beach, with two low benches on the lakeside where the captains, coaches and camp staff sit facing everyone else. Since Lake Manitouwabing has steep shores, the camp builders simply terraced the hill behind the beach, meaning that even those who sit near the back can see and hear pretty well. No one can roast marshmallows or anything, but this isn't that kind of fire.

Polly sits down next to me, and reaches over to squeeze my hand. Just sitting on this side is an accomplishment. Amy's arm is still looped through mine from the walk down here, and I can feel her shaking. After last year, her school has a lot to prove, and I can tell she's starting to feel it. We draw for order, Amy gets the first spot and I get the last one, and then begins an hour of self-doubt and goal setting that would set even the most practiced therapist's teeth on edge. The other teams talk about being afraid of heights or having too many new members. About being mocked as airheads instead of respected as athletes. About doing routines they'd slaved over to empty stands as everyone heads for the concessions. By the time I get up, I'm surprised half the campers haven't thrown themselves off the terrace and into the lake in despair. Polly gives my hand one more squeeze, and then I'm on my own, with the fire in front of me and the lake at my back.

"Palermo Heights Secondary School is famous for two things," I say. "Well, famous for one, infamous for the other. For a very small school in a slightly larger town, this is kind of an accomplishment. Usually, you need a school population in the four-digit range to merit any kind of attention. Of course, we're famous for our cheerleading. That's why we're here at this camp. Most of you have competed against us or seen us at exhibitions. You know we're unusually serious. Mighty, even though we're small." Across the campfire, I can see nods from the other teams. Our reputation has preceded us. I continue, "What you don't know, is that we're cursed."

Everyone's eyes are locked on me. I drop my voice so that I'm nearly whispering, and I feel the whole camp lean towards me.

"There's a girl from Palermo who isn't here tonight. Her name was Clara Abbey, and she sat beside me in grade six until Christmas break." Through the firelight, I see my teammates straighten in shock. They remember Clara, the grade twelves best of all. They remember Clara because Clara is a legend.

"I went to Florida that year with my family, and we didn't see the news," I continue. "It wasn't until I got back to school after break that I learned what happened. Clara had been coming home from her family's Christmas dinner when the car was struck by a drunk driver, and Clara was killed."

It's dead silent on the other side of the fire. No one knows where this story is going. Behind me, I can feel the staff and coaches shifting uncomfortably, wondering whether they should stop me. I don't look back, not even to see Polly's face. I don't have to. The teacher had rearranged the desks by lunchtime, and after that I sat next to Polly. It's how we became friends. We owe our friendship to Clara Abbey. Or the absence of Clara Abbey. That's why we wanted to tell her story, make her a real person instead of just a legend that gets whispered about in the hallways at school.

"That's our curse," I say. "Every single graduating class is one person short. Brian Wyn Davies, Charlotte Arbuckle, Adam Ouimette, Jack Chioran, Lindsay Carlson, and Clara Abbey. And those are just the ones I can remember. Every single class at Palermo Heights since 2006 has lost at least one student to a drunk driver."

The lake strikes in dissonant beats against the stones on the shore and the fire cracks. I know without a doubt that this is the best story ever told around this campfire. No one will top it, not in a million summers of cheer camp.

"But that's not all," I say. "We're cheerleaders. We understand spirit. We know how to make people feel it. And the spirit at Palermo Heights won't let us forget that a student has died." I have them where I want them. Now comes the tricky part. "Our challenge is more than remembering the classmate who died. Because every year one of the girls at PHSS gets pregnant. No one talks about that girl, not to her face at least, not in public." The audience giggles nervously. They weren't expecting that. "I'm not saying it's our punishment," I go on, "but I do think that it's life's way of reminding us that nothing should be taken for granted, that things might take a turn in ways that aren't fair or don't make sense." The giggle has run its course, and now the kids are back to wondering where the hell I'm going with this. I lean forward. "But here's an even better secret," I say. "We are going to break that curse. Clara Abbey died, it's true, but so far, no one has given birth. We have ten months until we graduate. Ten months to be smart. That is our challenge, and that is our goal. It's not exactly typical, I'll admit it, but it's ours."

There's a moment before anyone realizes that I'm done, and then scattered applause. I take my seat and look over at my coach. Caledon looks surprised, but also proud of me, and Polly grabs my hand again.

"Well, that was something different," whispers Amy. "Good for you."

"Thanks," I reply.

The camp director gets up and rather anticlimactically thanks us for our stories. We're asked to help one another in our quests, like we're headed for a volcano with a ring or something, and then we all get sent to bed.

"Remember, wake-up is at six thirty, so you're going to want to actually sleep," the director says.

I sigh. We'll be getting up well before six thirty. Half an hour really isn't enough time for twelve girls to turn themselves into cheerleaders. I remind myself to ask Amy if she wants to make a schedule or just hope that everyone cooperates.

"See you at breakfast," Polly says when we part ways. The boys have already crossed the field, Leo looking put out that I didn't let him kiss me in front of all the boys in his cabin. "Which, by the way, you'll be eating cold."

"After tonight," I tell her, "it will almost be worth it."

CHAPTER 4

I DREAM OF FLYING. On a good day, a basket toss gets me four metres or so of height. Crowds love the fast, complicated, gyroscopic stunts, but it's hard to see anything during those. So when I dream of flying, I dream of a simple back layout. When I dream of flying, everything is impossibly slow. When I uncurl my arms and throw my head back, there is no blur, no dizziness, and when I'm halfway around, head pointed straight down, I can see all my teammates. I have time to smile at them and see them smile back before the rotation carries me around and I float back into their arms. And then they are like a trampoline, because I'm back up in the air, higher this time. Again and again. Only sky above me and cheering crowds below. Again and again. I will never stop flying.

Except above me there is noise. Above me is not the sky. Above me is a farm kid, who never sleeps past the first whisper of morning and had volunteered to wake up the cabin. Mallory.

And then I'm awake. Amy and I decided last night that 5:50 was as late as we could all safely sleep and still be presentable for breakfast. I hear Mallory stir above, and the familiar creak of the bunk. I've got two more minutes at most before I need to make sure the new girls get this first morning right. They're going to need breakfast. There will be at least one hair-related emergency.

Two more minutes.

I keep my eyes closed and my sleeping bag tight under my chin. Will I ever have it this good again? I will wake up somewhere new this time next year. I have only a few more mornings in this world, in this world that loves me for what I love and for what I am good at.

One more minute. One more.

"How did Leo manage to get a van big enough for all of us?" Mallory asks as we make our own bunks. There's a knack to making top and bottom bunks simultaneously, and Mallory and I do it without a second thought. We're rushing because a couple of newbies had hair crises and now we're both behind.

"I don't know exactly, but when your dad owns a dealership, I guess you can make things happen with cars," I say, snapping a corner tight on my mattress. In truth I know very little about Leo's whole plan for the Saturday night of Labour Day weekend, beyond that he managed to convince Caledon that it would be excellent bonding for the "team leadership" to spend some extra time together before school starts, and to convince his father to find us a van big enough to fit the nine team members who will graduate at the end of the year.

"Well, however he pulled it off, I think it's great that you two are making it a team event. It's going to be fun." Mallory is done with her bed and is looking down at me as I fit my last corner.

"Yes. It'll be great." I smile back at her, and don't mention that I flat out refused to go at all, unless it *was* a team event. Camping out with Leo is pretty far down the list of things I want to do immediately after camp, but I am a cheerleader. I can get enthusiastic about anything.

Despite our best efforts, we are the eighth cabin selected for entry to breakfast. This is not as bad as it could be, of course, but it still means we spend fifteen minutes in line to be rewarded with rapidly cooling eggs. I'd opt for dry cereal, which is usually the safer bet, except I'm going to need all the protein I can get. The dining hall fills quickly, volume rising even after people start to eat. There's a hush around me, though, as everyone stares. I made quite an impact last night, apparently. There is enough space that we could sit as a cabin if we wanted to, but Leo is waving at me. After the campfire last night, the last thing I want to do is sit with strangers.

"Hey, Winters," he says as I take my seat and carefully arrange plate, cutlery and cup. "That was some story you told."

"It's not exactly a story," I tell him. "It's the truth."

"Yeah, but it still feels like a ghost story," Tig points out. "And telling it around a campfire in the middle of the woods doesn't help."

"Are you mad at me?" I ask. I put more salt on the eggs than I usually would.

"It might have been nice to have a heads-up," Leo says.

"Oh, come on," Tig says. "We do our part by not dying, and the girls do their part by not getting pregnant. How hard can it be?"

Carmen, who has taken a seat beside me, shoots Tig a withering look.

"What?" he demands.

"Last I checked, it takes two to tango," Carmen points out.

As they continue to snipe at each other, Leo leans closer to me. "But seriously, why didn't you tell me?" he asks.

"Polly and I talked about it," I say. "It was a captain thing. I didn't think you would care this much."

He looks offended, and I am not sure if it's because of Polly, because of the captain thing, or because I thought he wouldn't care. Leo always wants to talk, it seems, but never about the things that would make it easier to be his girlfriend.

"You basically told everyone that girls shouldn't have sex," he says.

"I told everyone to be careful. Speaking of, I really didn't appreciate your addition to my suitcase."

"Hey, that would be being careful," he drawls, but he still looks hurt.

"Look," I say, trying to mend fences. I think about putting

my hand on his arm, or something, but I need both hands to eat, and we're on the clock. "Tig's right, in a way. The not-dying part is equal opportunity. I bet you can remember all the girls who had babies. Can you name any of the fathers?"

"I still don't see why it had to be a secret," Leo persists.

I roll my eyes. "We were worried that if Caledon found out, she'd tell us we couldn't do it," I snap. It's louder than I intended, and both Tig and Carmen look at us. "But now it's done, and she supports us, and I don't see why you can't too."

"Fine, fine," he says, turning back to his breakfast. He smirks, that studied expression I think he means to be attractive. "I totally understand keeping secrets from Caledon."

It hangs there, a fight we could have right here in the middle of the dining hall if I want to pick it with him. If I don't, he'll assume I'm relenting. If I do, it'll be a spectacle. I wish Polly were here. She is so much better at figuring this sort of thing out, even though she's never dated anyone at all.

"Whatever," I say, choosing the high road. Leo smiles, but when he would have put his arm around my shoulder, I duck away and stand up. "I'm going outside to stretch before we get our session assignments."

I finish my eggs on the way to the plate return, and take the sausage and potato cake out with me, wrapped in a napkin. I've had about as much of Leo as I can stand, and we haven't even gotten started yet. Maybe we'll be in different groups for the week. They like to split up schools, so it's a definite possibility.

I'm not the only one who has chosen to finish breakfast on the grass. It's wet from the dew, but drying fast. I finish my breakfast, tossing the napkin into one of the garbage cans placed on the field, and stretch while a couple of boys do hand-stands beside me. They're shirtless, of course, so I'm not sure what school they're from. But they're laughing, and I can't resist the challenge, so I join in, easily outlasting the pair of them before collapsing in a heap.

"What's your name?" asks one of them.

"Hermione," I say.

Before I can ask their names, the throng of cheerleaders exits the dining hall, and our separate teams sweep us off. Leo's still glowering and I don't think seeing me in the grass with those guys helped, but I don't have time to think of anything but the days ahead. Through the crowd, I see Polly's face: set and ready to go. I do my best to marshal my own features the same, chan-nelling all the determination and confidence I can muster. Show-time. Last time.

My time.

CHAPTER 5

THE NEXT WEEK PASSES IN a blur of acrobatics, jumps into the lake and napping at every possible opportunity. We lose two or three people a day to heat exhaustion, and probably regular exhaustion too, but those of us who have done this before push through. Fatigue here has a different quality. It's hard work shared in common with more people than just your own. I've leaned on shoulders I don't know, and been held steady in the air by the hands of people I've just met. My own shoulder is braced with bright pink Kinesio tape, expertly applied at breakfast by a St. Ig's girl who saw me get dropped the day before. It's everything I've hoped for, and the smiles that greet me in the mess hall or on the field are even better than I'd dreamed.

—

By Friday night, which is movie night, we're all completely ready to drop. Tomorrow is technically our day off, but since it's the only day we'll have to practice our final routine for the exhibition at the end of the next week, Polly and I won't be relaxing too much.

They've erected a huge screen on the field for us, and once the sun sets, we all set up camp in the grass. It's been a dry summer, or this would be very uncomfortable. I can tell Amy wants to come sit with us. I think there's a lot more bitterness on her team than she's letting on. I've promised Polly though, and we do have a lot of work to do. Anyway, by now I think I've seen just about every happy sports movie there is, and when *Rudy* starts up, flickering on the giant white screen, I know I'm not going to miss anything.

"Hey," says Leo, slumping into the grass beside me. "Haven't seen much of you all week."

It's true. It's a full week, and I haven't had a lot of time for socializing—or maybe I haven't made a lot of time. Also, Amy turns out to be really good at improv, so our mealtime cheers put us consistently at the front of the pack. We can usually manage to save one seat for Polly, but after that things get awkward. "I've been busy," I tell him, which is also the truth. I've never had a boyfriend at camp before, and it's turning out to be really hard. "Though if it makes you feel better, I've been able to do some quality spying on St. Ig's."

I mean it as a joke, but even in the dark I can tell Leo isn't close to laughing.

"St. Ig's?" he says. He puts his arm around my shoulder, but instead of being sweet it feels possessive. "You're on pet name status with them? Do the St. Ig's boys call you Winters yet? I notice their cabin busts its ass to make sure they're in for meals with yours."

"Don't be silly," I say, leaning away from him. "My cabin has half their team in it. Or course they try to sit with us. And nobody calls me Winters but you."

"Don't you forget it," he says. He's trying to joke now too, and even though it isn't working, I laugh.

"If you're extra nice to me, I'll tell you what I've learned," I say, smiling at him.

But Leo just rolls his eyes, and looks towards the screen.

I'm not a moron; on some level, I know people come to this camp for reasons other than mine. And I know that most people don't understand what these two weeks mean to me. But Polly and I have worked too hard to not take advantage of every chance we get, particularly when we know it will be the last shot we have. I know this is the last year, that next summer will be the first different summer I've had in more than half a decade. It will be the first summer I am not a cheerleader. It makes me even more determined to squeeze whatever I can out of these days at camp.

"Ugh, *Rudy*." Polly sighs as she drops in next to me on the grass, and rests her head on my shoulder. In theory, there are dozens of inspirational sports movies, but my practical experience would indicate otherwise. We've all seen this one more times than we care to count. It doesn't matter, though, because we have a lot of work to do. Or at least work I would like to do. Long before we've made as much progress as I'd hoped for, Tig gets restless, and Polly has to take him to task for wasting what little time we have to work on this together.

Leo bristles and puts his arm around me again. He hits Polly accidentally because she's been leaning on me to see over my shoulder and he'd moved too fast for her to get out of the way. "Hermione might be stuck spying on St. Ig's next week too. This might be the last chance we get to plan."

"You could spy on whoever you're bunking with," Polly offers as I pull the whiteboard out of my sleeping bag.

While everyone around us watches Rudy lust over the Notre Dame football team, we sketch out formations and double-check the count to make sure they're physically possible. Leo assures me that Dion and Cameron, our two new boys, can handle anything I throw at them. Still, this will be the first time we work together. It's hard to trust a completely new person to catch you, but if Leo tells me they can, I believe him. Every time I'm tempted to put them on the sidelines, I force myself to put them back in the thick of it.

"Hey," comes a whispered voice behind me, and all four of us jump. I turn around, and it's Amy with a bunch of the St. Ig's kids. For the first time, she looks happy to be hanging out with them. "Sorry!" she says. "We're sneaking down to the lake. Wanna come?"

I look at Polly, who can smell an intersquad prank a mile away. I have no problem getting tp'ed or ending up with Jell-O in my shoes for the cause, but unauthorized time at the lake has serious, dish-washing-related repercussions. Polly seems torn, but finally shakes her head.

"Sorry," I say. "But we've got a lot of planning to do. Plus, Leo always cries at the end of this movie, and it's one of the only times I get to see him be vulnerable." I know as soon as I've said it that I've made a horrible mistake. Leo's arm tightens on my shoulder, and I can hear Tig laughing.

"We'll come," Leo says, letting go of me and pulling Tig to his feet. Tig grumbles, but he's powerless to resist Leo.

"Leo," I hiss, trying to convey that Polly thinks it might be a prank without actually saying the words out loud.

"Hey," he says. "We're here to make friends and influence people, aren't we?" He throws an arm around Amy's shoulder. He's trying for an effect that he's not quite achieving, and I don't think I'm the only one cringing.

Amy is looking at her shoes. I know that this is an awful idea, but I can't stop him without being a jerk.

"They'll be fine," Polly says, and I back down. If Polly thinks the St. Ig's team is on the up-and-up, then they probably are. And if they're not, it's not like Leo's new to pranks.

"Be safe," I say, which is also dumb, but it's the only thing I can think of.

"He'll be fine," says one of the St. Ig's boys. "It's not like drowning is part of your curse."

Everyone laughs at that, and then everyone stops laughing really quickly so we don't accidentally get the attention of an adult. Then they all melt into the darkness towards the lake.

It isn't until Amy sits down next to me that I realize she hasn't gone all the way to the lake with them. I'm a bit confused, because she'd invited us in the first place, but maybe she only wanted to do the prank if we were going too.

"Do you want me to leave so you can do choreo?" she asks.

"No, we can't do much more without the guys," Polly says. "And as you can see, they have the attention spans of gerbils."

"At least yours listen when you talk," Amy says.

"Appointed captain, eh?" Polly says. We were elected—unanimously—so we have our jobs because the team wanted us to have them.

"By the vice principal," Amy confirms.

"Oooooh, you're practically a narc!" I hope she understands I'm teasing, and when she laughs, I feel much better about it.

"Don't remind me," she says. And I can see that her laugh hides real distress.

"Will you guys be okay next week?" Polly asks.

After our "day off" tomorrow, we launch into five straight days of endurance and strength training. It's equal parts cardio, choreo, and hell, all leading up to our performance day on Friday. It's an incredibly exhausting week in every sense, and I've seen it bring even strong teams to tears. At least I'll be leading a team I *know* has my back. Amy might as well be carrying a picnic basket of vipers.

For a few moments there's silence and we each pretend to watch the movie. I cannot imagine the dread Amy's feeling for next week. It's the exact opposite of what I have.

"Maybe it'll bring us all together? Make us stronger for the season?" Amy breaks our silence but she doesn't sound hopeful.

"I've heard war does that to people," Polly says. "And as you know, cheerleading is a lot like war."

She sounds so serious that I can't help laughing.

Polly keeps going, as if to prove Amy isn't the only one good at improv. "Or is there any chance you might contract a fatal illness?" She nods at Rudy in his Notre Dame uniform. "You know, 'Win one for the Gipper'? Nothing better for team spirit than a captain's life cut tragically short." Polly reaches over and holds her hand against Amy's forehead, and Amy swoons theatrically, nearly falling into her arms across my lap. "You are feeling a bit feverish."

And then Amy's laughing too, even though it's a very serious part of the movie, and everyone is looking back at us. We ignore them, still piled on top of one another, and laugh until we cry. The moment is well and truly broken when a very, very wet Leo grabs Amy by her shoulders and pulls her out of Polly's grasp.

"Leo!" I say. "What the fuck are you doing?"

"She set us up!" Leo hisses. At least he's smart enough not to shout. If he gets caught, it will be obvious where he's been.

"She's been here the whole time," I hiss. Polly has got up and gone around me to make sure that Amy is okay. She seems mostly surprised, but I am shaking with anger. "And anyway, you can't just walk up here and grab a girl like that. What's wrong with you?"

"Of course you'd defend them," Leo says. "All they do is talk about how awesome you are. How you're a real captain—with real legs to match."

Both Amy and I flinch at that, but Polly goes ice cold.

"Leon David McKenna." Polly is glaring at him, her face so hard that even I'm scared of her, just for a second. "Get your ass to your cabin before you get caught, and if I *ever* hear you talk like that about any girl, alive or dead, I will skin you."

Leo looks like he has about a million things to say, but he says none of them. He slinks off through the grass. I have no idea where Tig went. I hope he's smart and just went straight to his cabin to dry off.

"What was that about?" asks Jenny, who has appeared out of nowhere. I don't know how much she's heard, and right now I kind of don't care.

"Leo got pranked and he's pissed about it," I tell her as calmly as I can manage, though I can feel my heart racing. Everyone is looking at us again, more interested than when we were laughing. Scandal, even the potential of, attracts the worst kind of attention, and right now that's the last thing we need. "It's really important that no one cause a scene."

Jenny goes back to watching the movie, and I turn to Amy. "I am so sorry about that."

"I had no idea," she says. "They never tell me anything."

"Were any of them from our cabin?"

"No," she says. "They all love you. It was the boys and the other girls."

"Well, thank goodness for small blessings," Polly says. "And as much as I hate to say it, I think the coaches just got here. We're going to have to watch the movie."

I look up and see the familiar silhouette of Caledon. I don't know how she does it, but she always seems able to see us in the dark. Hopefully Leo and Tig will count themselves out for the rest of the night. They don't care about the triumphant finish in this movie anyway. Neither of them has ever been a benchwarmer in their lives.

"Agreed," I say.

I don't remember the last time I went to a movie and some-one sat between Polly and me. If it had to be anyone, I'm glad it's Amy. I don't usually get sentimental about camp friendships, largely because I've never had one, but when we all go back home next week, I think I'm going to miss her.

CHAPTER 6

THEY DON'T DROP US, BUT the new boys are slow. In theory, you can be a cheerleader if you can count to eight, but Cameron and Dion are lost without music. We can only go as fast as our slowest teammates, and at practice on Saturday morning, Dion and Cameron are by far the slowest. I can tell Caledon is getting to the end of her patience.

"Dion, Cameron," I say, taking pity on them. "Come here for a moment."

I'm pretty sure that part of their problem is that they're lifting Jenny. She's the lightest (a fact she's quite proud of), but she's also the least stable in the air, and the boys are compensating for her and losing their count.

"Watch Leo and Tig do it," I say once they've joined me on the sideline.

Polly counts them through the whole thing. They don't need it, but Cameron and Dion do. We watch Leo lift Polly into Tig's grasp, and then Tig braces himself and throws her up in the air. She flips, perfectly in time and still counting. There's a moment when she hangs in the air, just her and the sky and the very tops of the trees. The view is great, if you can keep your head together, and that is something both Polly and I excel at. She comes all the way around and descends, and the boys catch her and put her on her feet for the eight count.

"Goddamn." Cameron shakes his head and wipes the sweat from his eyes. "I should have stuck with hockey."

"Hockey's too easy," I say, trying to radiate patience and confidence. "Your turn."

Polly takes over the main practice, shifting Jenny to the dance line for the moment while I practice the throw. Cameron is the stronger of the two, but Dion is more sure, so he's the one who will be throwing me.

"Five, six, seven, eight!" I count, rocking back on my feet and throwing myself into Cameron's arms.

He's smart enough to use the inertia to get me towards Dion, but he pushes just a bit too hard, so when Dion throws me up in the air, I go off behind him instead of straight up. In the air, there's not a lot I can do to save myself, so I finish the flip and point my feet to the ground. I do my best not to panic, but I can't see the ground for most of the manoeuver.

"Shit!" curses Dion, who realizes his mistake almost as soon as I am out of his hands.

He's backpedaling frantically and Cameron moves with him.

When I come around and see that they're going to catch me after all, I tuck. It's still too late. All three of us crash to the ground in some dreadful kind of sandwich. Dion has taken one for the team and is on the bottom, but Cameron is on top of me, and it's hard to breathe.

"Hermione!" Leo has broken formation and is pulling Cameron off me while Cam is too stunned to move.

"I'm good, I'm good!" I call out. "Dion?"

"Ooof," he grunts. I think I've elbowed him in the gut. I hope that's where it was, anyway. With Cameron on top of me, it's not like I have much control. "Cameron, you weigh a tonne."

"Tell me about it," I joke as we extricate arms and legs. Dion's blushing and does his best to push me up while also not touching me anymore than he already is.

"It's all muscle," Cameron says, and I know, at least, that his ego survived the fall.

"You're all in one piece, then?" asks Caledon, who looks concerned even though we're laughing.

"Yes, Coach!" we chorus.

Then I clap my hands, and shout, "Dion, Cameron. Let's get it right. One more time." They snap into position and I count, "Five, six, seven, eight!"

"Are you sure you're okay?" Dion says an hour later when we head back out after lunch. I know he feels awful, but it was a legitimate mistake. If it had been a stupid one, I might be less forgiving.

"It's fine, Dion," I tell him. "The important thing is that you caught me. As long as you do that, we're okay."

I sling my arm around his shoulder, which is a reach because he's a lot taller than I am, and when I stumble from trying to walk off balance, he picks me up and swings me around his neck. I shriek, even though I know it's in good fun, and we're both smiling when he sets me down.

"God, Winters," Leo says, appearing beside me. He's spent most of the lunch break fussing over me, and had gone to get tape. "Be careful!"

"We're fine," I say. "We've got to trust one another, or the team won't work."

"You could just trust me," he mumbles.

"I'm the captain." I stop walking so we can have a chance at doing this privately. "We talked about this before we got on the bus back in Palermo. You agreed."

"I know," he says. "I just miss having you to myself."

I don't tell him that he's never had me to himself, because that would only hurt his feelings. We've only been dating since nationals last spring, and even though we've spent a lot of time together over the summer, he hardly has a monopoly on my heart. I like him, obviously, or I wouldn't be dating him, but I like Polly too, and she's been my friend for much longer. What Leo and I have is exciting and new. What Polly and I have is forever. But Leo doesn't seem to understand that and worse, he never seems to try.

By two thirty, when the weather turns from superhot to *su-per*hot, we are cheered out. At this time of year, the days start cool enough that we show up in long pants and sweatshirts, but after lunch everyone is stripped down to shorts and T-shirts or tank tops. We're also the last team left on the field, by about fifteen minutes. That's what makes us Fighting Bears, Caledon tells us: We don't stop until we're done. Once we've done the routine three times with no foul-ups, she dismisses us. The boys run straight to the lake, shuck their shirts and dive in. We girls drag ourselves to our cabins, change into suits and grab our towels. Most of the team is splashing around in the deep part of the swimming area, but the idea of treading water is more than I can cope with, so I just go in to my knees and sit down. My suit immediately fills with sand. It is a distinctly childish feeling, and I don't actually hate it.

"Well, at least no one died." Polly sits down next to me, and for a moment I'm tempted to dunk her, but there's no way I'm winning that, and we both know it, so I settle for running my hands through the water instead.

"It wasn't that bad, or Caledon would still have us up there," I point out.

"True," Polly says. "The boys did well and I think the Sarahs have improved dramatically since their tryouts."

"Haven't they done anything that earns them a nickname yet?" I ask. It's getting a bit ridiculous.

"I think one of them is trying out 'Digger,'" Polly says. "But I don't know which one."

"Great," I say. "They'll end up called Pom-Poms or something, and then we'll be really screwed."

"Yes," Polly agrees sagely. "Our biggest problem will almost certainly be our inability to tell the Sarahs apart."

I giggle, and Polly grins. I recognize danger half a second too late, and she dunks me before I can put up a fight. I come up spluttering, because I was still laughing when I went under. I know better than to try to return more of the same, so I splash in her general direction.

"That's weak, Winters," Leo says, from the dock, watching me again. "Do you want me to dunk her for you?"

"It would be the last thing you ever did," I tell him. "And we need you too badly to lose you this early in the season."

He laughs, and then Tig does a cannonball right beside us. The splash isn't much, because the water's so shallow, and he comes up howling from a stubbed toe, which cracks the rest of us up.

It's the last time we have for fun and laughing for the next six days, though, because starting at seven a.m. on Sunday morning, the real work starts. It gets a bit cooler as the week drags on, reminding us that Labour Day weekend waits for us on Friday, and school after that, but we don't really notice that the temperature has dropped. During the day, we're working too hard, and at night, we're dead to the world.

Cheerleaders have to be in excellent shape, and by the final Friday night, we're all in stupendous form. The trainers let us knock off half an hour early so that some of us can shower before dinner. Amy and I let the younger girls go first, and we show up to the dining hall sweaty and gross. It's worth it, though, because in the forty minutes it takes us to eat, the hot water replenishes itself, and we can take slightly longer showers as a result.

When I get back into the cabin, there are clothes everywhere.

Thank goodness there's no inspection tomorrow. The girls are trading back and forth; outfits and hair accessories and makeup tips. You'd think it was something more important than an end-of-camp dance where the girls outnumber the boys four to one. And I have a boyfriend, of course. Still, I have to admit, I'm a little excited myself, and can't stop smiling as I shake out the sundress I packed for the occasion. After a week of eight counts and dance numbers where everyone's arms and legs do exactly what they're supposed to, all at the same time, it'll be a relief to just let loose and dance for the fun of it.

"Here," says Amy, gesturing to the bed in front of her. "I'll do your hair."

She's not the wizard Polly is, but she's still pretty good. In the end, my hair is a lattice of alternating colours and I can't follow one lock from start to finish. It's going to take me an hour to pull out, but everyone in the cabin will be in the same boat, so I don't mind.

"Your turn!" I say, and we switch places. I'm no master either, but Amy's thrilled when she sees herself in the mirror.

"Hermione!" Mallory shouts. "We're going to be late!"

"You're supposed to be late," Jenny tells her.

I suddenly remember that Leo wanted to meet at the doors before the dance. Too late for that now. I wince a little at the thought of another black mark on my girlfriend record, but then Amy grabs my hand and I can't bring myself to care.

By the time we get to the dining hall, which has been completely emptied of tables, the overhead lights are out, and the bass and a strobe are pumping. I spot Polly in the centre of the crowd and she is a thing of fearsome beauty. Unconstrained by choreography, Polly is one of those dancers a circle inevitably forms around. She is a tiny thing with huge gravity. I stop in my tracks and watch as her every move is captured by the strobe.

Whoever's playing DJ screeches the song to a halt, and abruptly launches into one of those decades-old power-pop anthems that demands ironic chorus shouting. I am more than happy to join in. Apparently I really cannot get enough group shouting.

A song later, Polly grabs my hands and pulls me into the seething mass. It's all limbs and hips and shoulders and hair, and then someone puts the cup in my hand. It's hot and I'm thirsty, so I drain it and go looking for a garbage can to put the empty cup in.

"Hey," says a voice I don't quite recognize amidst all the noise. A boy's voice. "Looking for something?"

"The garbage," I say. "Have you seen it?"

There's something wrong. I wasn't this tired until right this second. I shouldn't be so tired. I should find Polly. Polly will know how tired I am supposed to be.

"It's this way," he says. He leads me away from the dining hall, where I know the garbage isn't. For some reason, I can't tell him that he's going the wrong way.

There's a moment when I know that I should scream. But screaming would be hard. And blackness would be easy.

Black picks me.

PART 2

Why, this would make a man of salt to use his eyes
for garden waterpots. Ay, and laying autumn's dust.

CHAPTER 7

I'VE NEVER SEEN POLLY'S FACE so white. I've never felt this rough waking up, either. I can't remember what we did, why she's so worried, but it must be awful. I hope we don't get expelled. Also, I am going to vomit.

The nurse is there as soon as I heave and has me sitting up and puking into a small tin pan almost before I realize what I'm doing. I'm vaguely impressed with my accuracy, to be honest. It's not a big pan. Maybe the nurse is just really good at this. I don't remember why I'm sick. I don't even feel that sick. I just feel . . . completely wrong.

"Oh God, Hermione!" Polly breathes. She hasn't let go of my hand, even though vomit is the one thing in this world she can't stand the sight of. Whatever this is, it must be bad.

"What happened?" I ask.

Polly and the nurse exchange a glance, and the nurse shakes her head. I realize that I am very naked under the blanket and hospital gown, and that I seem to have pulled a muscle in my thigh. Or maybe my abdomen. It's not something I've ever pulled before, and I've strained almost every muscle I have at one point or another in my cheerleading career.

"You remember nothing?" the nurse says. She is being so careful. I wonder if this is what it's like to feel fragile. I have never in my life been fragile. She passes me a drink of water, and I take a mouthful before she lets me back onto the pillow. Everything is heavy and the light hurts my eyes.

"We were at the dance," I say. "I was with Polly." There's something missing. Something important. "No," I say. "I wasn't with Polly. I had an empty cup, and I was looking for the garbage and then . . ."

It's blank. It's blank for about ten seconds, and then it stops being blank very quickly.

Polly grabs my other hand and the heart monitor they've got me hooked up to beeps at a frantic pace. I can't breathe. I can't breathe. I left the dance with a boy I didn't know and I can't breathe.

"Honey, honey," the nurse says. "He's not here. You breathe with Polly, okay? You breathe with Polly and no talking. When you think you can handle some questions, there's an officer—a female officer—and your coach ready to talk to you."

"Her parents are in Europe. Vacation," Polly says. "I can't remember if we told you that."

"Your coach is taking care of it," the nurse says, and I will never forget the look she gives Polly before she says, "You just hold her hands."

"Polly," I say. And then I can't stop saying it. "Polly Polly PollyPollyPolly." I'm near hysteria, I can feel it. I'm going to scream and scream and scream, to make up for the screaming I didn't do last night. I am going to pull my skin off and grind it into the floor and then I'm going to cry until I've got nothing left.

I don't do any of those things, though, because Polly climbs right into bed with me. She can move so fast. The nurse doesn't even have time to protest. She's on top of the blanket, and her legs are on top of mine, but her arms are around me, keeping me from flying apart, and suddenly I want to die slightly less than I did the moment before.

"Breathe," she orders, and we do.

We breathe for a whole minute. And then two. And then three. After five, Polly sits up a bit. I make an absolutely broken sound, and she kisses me on the forehead.

"I am getting up now," she says. "And I am getting Caledon and the officer. And you are going to breathe and talk. And then we're going to eat Jell-O. And then you can cry some more, okay?"

I nod.

"Say it," she says.

"I am going to breathe and talk, and then we're going to eat Jell-O, and then I can cry," I parrot obediently. I think I mean it.

"Well done," the nurse whispers as Polly takes her seat. "Officer? She's ready."

I can tell that Caledon wants to rush in, pick me up, and

make sure I'm okay. She stays outside of my personal space, though, and I'm so grateful for the breathing room that I want to vomit again, except I've got nothing left.

The officer is in plainclothes. There probably aren't a lot of female officers in the Ontario Provincial Police north of Barrie. I wonder how far she's come from. She's taller than I am, which is not hard, and shorter than Caledon. She's also much stockier. She looks like you'd need a bulldozer to knock her over. She's not young, particularly, but there's a sense of newness to her that makes me wonder how long she has been a police officer.

"Hello, Hermione," she says.

I wonder if she's a Harry Potter fan, like my dad, or a Greek myth groupie, like my mother. Or if she just got lucky reading my name off the report, and pronouncing it correctly was a fluke. I shake my head and force myself to pay attention.

"My name is Officer Plummer," she says. "You can call me Caroline if you like."

Maybe I am supposed to say something? All I can think is how I can't quite figure out how she might fit into a routine. Maybe she's a base? I don't know what to say, which is awful, because I always know what to say. I am not fragile and I know what to say.

She pushes on. "If you need to stop for any reason, you just tell me, okay?"

"Okay," I say, and then because I can't stop myself I add, "Polly promised me I can cry later if I talk now."

"That's a good plan." Officer Plummer must be a real pro because I sound like a moron and she isn't even cracking a smile. "Can you tell me what you had for dinner on Friday?"

"Pizza," I say without hesitating. "We went in seventh, so all that was left was vegetarian and Hawaiian, and it was cold."

"Good," says Officer Plummer when Polly nods. "Then what did you do?"

"Amy and I had volunteered to shower last," I tell her. "The others thought we were doing them a favour, but really we just wanted warm water. We took our showers, and then Amy did my hair."

I remember my hair. It had been beautiful and intricate. I touch my head, and then I wish I hadn't.

"I'll comb it out later," Polly quickly promises.

"Did you go to the dance with Amy?" Officer Plummer asks.

"Yes," I say. "And Mallory—another girl from Palermo. Everyone else had gone ahead by then."

"What happened when you arrived?"

This part is harder, blurrier. I try to make the memories sharpen into focus.

"Polly was already there," I say. "She pulled me into the middle of the dance floor. We're very good dancers. Even in a room full of people who dance competitively. It was fun." The lack of clarity in my memory shows in my voice. It's quiet and static, a far cry from my usual range. I can only think enough for short sentences.

"Do you remember who was with you?" Officer Plummer isn't taking notes, I notice, but then I see the recorder in her pocket.

"No. It was crowded and hot, like a mosh pit or something."
I have no idea what a mosh pit is like, but it seemed as good a comparison as any.

"What happened next?"

"Someone gave me a drink and I drank it," I say. "And then I went to find the recycling, but I was tired."

Polly winces.

"I can't breathe," I say. "I mean, I can't remember. And I can't find the garbage or Polly. But I do find a guy."

"What does he look like?" Officer Plummer sounds hopeful. I suppose I've been doing well up to this point.

"I don't know," I tell her after a moment. I am good at colours, but faces always stream together. I remember Polly's face, and Amy's, and my own team, but the others—I didn't even try. It is my last camp. No, *was.* I was thinking about other things. "I can get that far, but it was dark, and I don't know. I know what must have happened next, but I don't remember getting there."

"That's a side effect of the drug you were given," the nurse says. She seems caught between wanting to step towards me, to take care of me, and staying as close to the door as she can, and still do her job. "I'm sorry, honey."

"Will her memories come back?" Polly asks.

"I'm not really an expert at this," Officer Plummer admits. "I'm mostly here because . . ."

She stops talking, but we all know how the sentence ends. We're in the middle of nowhere, far away from the officers who have been trained for this, and she was probably the only female on duty when the call came in.

"It's okay," I tell her. "You're okay."

"You call me," she says, passing over her card. "You call me if you remember anything, or if you need to talk, okay?"

Polly puts the card on the table next to the Jell-O, and the officer leaves. Caledon and the nurse exchange a look, and then Caledon steps a bit closer. "Do you want all the details, Hermione?" she asks. I've never heard her sound so scared and unsure.

"Can I have them from Polly?" I whisper. I'm so pathetic, but if I hear it from grown-ups it will be worse.

"Of course," she says. "But there's one more thing." She hesitates for a long moment, and then takes a deep breath. "They couldn't do a full ess ay ee kay for you," she says, and it takes me a moment to process that she's saying some sort of acronym. "Polly can explain the details, if you like, but the evidence left on you was contaminated. The tech was concerned that with the water, the DNA profile won't be complete."

I've watched enough crime shows to know that something is always left behind. I scratched him or he licked me or something. But if Caledon says it, it must be the truth.

"Oh," I say. I'm not sure what else I *can* say. Polly will be better at the details. She always is.

Caledon picks up a small plastic cup from the tray. It was on the other side of the Jell-O, so I hadn't seen it until now.

"This is an emergency contraceptive," she says. The pills rattle against the plastic. Her hands are shaking.

"Polly, help me sit up," I say. "Will they make me sick?"

"A bit," the nurse says, "but you'll be here the whole time."

Polly pours more water and passes me the cups. I down the pills quickly, and then lie back down.

"I'll be just outside," Caledon says.

"Where's Florry?" I ask. "And the team?"

"I've sent them home," Caledon says. "They're okay. You just shout if you need me."

"Here's the call bell," the nurse says, indicating where it's been clipped to my bed. "Press the red button, and I'll be along."

And then we're alone, Polly and me. I realize that I'm not even sure where we are, though I assume it's the hospital in Parry Sound. Polly hands me my Jell-O and I eat it mechanically. When I've finished, she climbs back into bed with me, and I curl on my side so that we're face-to-face like we used to do when we had sleepovers as children and had to whisper because we were supposed to be sleeping and the adults were only a wall away.

"I need you to say it, Polly," I whisper. It will be real as soon as she does, but there's no one better at pulling off Band-Aids than Polly Olivier.

"They found you in the lake," she says, her shining eyes inches from mine. "Amy did, I mean, when you weren't at the cabin when she got back. She was frantic. You were still in your dress, but your underwear was gone, and you were up to your waist in water, lying on the rocks."

"Stop stalling, Polly." I'm not even sure who is talking anymore. SAEK. *Sexual Assault something something.* Our hands find each other's, and I know now I won't fly apart.

She closes her eyes for a second, and the shining leaks out as tears. Then she forces them open again. "Someone spiked your drink at the dance. And then he got you alone and took you down by the water. And you couldn't stop him, because the bastard drugged you. And then he raped you."

She never hesitates, my Polly. She just rips it right off. She never cries, either. Not usually. But this time we lie together in the hospital bed and I can't tell whose tears are whose.

CHAPTER 8

I DREAM ABOUT CLARA ABBEY, which I haven't done in years. She's still eleven in my dream, swinging by her ankles from the monkey bars at recess. It's not graceful, not the way she does it. She loves to be up high, but she's grown faster than the rest of us have. She's tall and not sure where the ends of her arms and legs are. I can twist myself around the bars, flipping and contorting like a trapeze artist, but Clara can only hang. She never learns how to deal with her height. She'll be hanging there forever.

"So will you," she tells me. Her voice is strained and her face is red from being upside down. "They'll talk about both of us forever, now. It won't matter what else you do."

"No," I tell her. "I won't let it. I won't let them."

"You can't control it," she says. "You can't control the other cars. You just have to keep driving and hope for the best."

"Who are we talking about?" I ask. "You or me?"

"It doesn't matter," she says. "We're the same now. Two more numbers on the scorecard."

I flip over the bar next to her, and for a moment we hang beside each other. The bell rings, and the playground starts to empty. The real Clara would have pushed herself off the bars and landed heavily on the ground as soon as the bell sounded. This one doesn't move. She's stuck on the monkey bars because some moron drove drunk on Christmas Day. I start to push off, heading for the ground, but I get stuck halfway around.

"No!" I shout at the empty yard. The door shuts. Everyone has moved on and left us behind. "NO!"

And then Polly is shaking me, and I am awake.

"Nightmare?" She hands me the water and I take a sip.

"Kind of," I say. "More disturbing than scary."

"Want to talk about it?"

"No," I say. "What time is it?"

"Nearly eleven o'clock," she says, glancing at her watch. "And it's Sunday, if you were curious."

"I had figured that out myself, actually." I'm not trying to be funny, but I'm in serious laugh-or-cry mode right now. "On account of the sunlight streaming through the windows."

Polly shrugs, but does me the courtesy of smiling a little bit. Yesterday evening passed in a blur of painful cramping from the emergency contraceptives, and I cried so much that I had a headache. They didn't sedate me, for which I'm glad, so I hadn't expected to sleep that long.

My parents aren't getting in until Monday evening, so Caledon put most of our equipment on the bus and is going to drive Polly and me back to Palermo in the van herself. My parents must be absolutely miserable. Being on a plane is bad enough.

There's a knock on the door, and Polly looks to me for a moment to make sure I'm ready for people. I nod.

"Come in," she says.

It's Officer Plummer again. This time she's in uniform, her hair all secured under her hat. She does not look like someone I would want to mess with. When she comes through the door, she takes her hat off and tucks it under her arm. I wonder if there are rules for that, or if she's just hot.

"Sorry to disturb you again," she says.

"It's okay," I say. It isn't, but it's not like I can get very much more disturbed.

Officer Plummer swallows. I know instantly that she's been practicing all day the speech she's about to give me. Probably in the car. Probably in the elevator. Probably in her head right now. And it never gets any better. I do my best not to panic, which is harder than it used to be.

"Miss Winters," she says, apparently deciding that formality will make whatever this is easier, hopefully for both of us. "As you know, the physical evidence on you was compromised by your time in the lake."

She makes it sound like I went swimming. I wonder what the criminal charge for "dropping an unconscious person in the lake" is.

"Therefore, it was decided that no samples were to be collected from the male campers and staff at Camp Manitou-wabing." I know that already, but it still feels hopeless. Part of me is glad: No samples means no charges, no trial, no thinking about this once I go home. Part of me, the part that sounds like Polly, is fighting mad.

"However," she continues. "Should the results of your pregnancy test be positive, and should you wish to share that with the Ontario Provincial Police, we will have reason to take those samples, and run the tests when the pregnancy has . . ." Her professionalism fails her and she deflates. "I'm really sorry, Miss Winters," she says, shoulders rounding forward. "You deserve much better than this."

"Honestly, the fact that this isn't old hat to you makes me feel like there's some hope left," I tell her. It's a slight exaggeration, but it costs me nothing. I like to know that I can still give. "We don't have that result yet."

"Do you still have my card?" Plummer asks.

"Maybe," I say. "Though it might have gotten a bit crumpled yesterday." I'd lost track of holding it after everyone left and Polly got back into bed with me. I think at one point, one of us might have tried to use it for Kleenex.

"I'll leave another," she says, and fishes it out of the pocket next to her gun. She puts it on the table. "Call me if you decide to move ahead with the investigation."

I nod again, and even though she has been nothing but helpful, I suddenly want her to leave as fast as possible. She takes a few more seconds to ask Polly if we need anything, but Caledon has already gone shopping for us, and then Officer Plummer goes. When we're alone, pretending privacy even though the doorway to the hall is open, I take several deep breaths.

"Well?" Polly asks when I have regained control of myself.

"I don't know," I tell her. I think about my dream, about Clara telling me that I'll complete the card. Is that my subconscious way of telling me that I will be the class pregnancy? Is it the drugs and the emotional cocktail burning through my system?

"Don't you want to catch him?" Polly asks.

"Yes," I say. "But think about what that *means*."

It hangs between us for about five seconds before Polly's eyes widen and she realizes what she's accidentally wished for.

"I didn't mean . . . ," she starts, and then stops.

"I know," I tell her. "I know exactly what you meant. And I do want him caught. I just can't think about it until I have to."

"You know that either way, any way, I'm with you, right?" she says.

"I do," I tell her. "And believe me, I will probably take full advantage of that."

"I just . . . I feel so bad that I didn't notice," she says. "I was right beside you."

"He was very smart about it," I say. She flinches. I'm past flinching. "I mean, if I'd stayed with you, we would have thought I was tired, and Amy would have taken me back to the cabin. He waited until I left the group, and I was only going to the garbage cans."

"I still feel terrible," she says. "And Amy feels awful. She had a full-on panic attack after the ambulance took you away. I couldn't stay, because Caledon was leaving to follow in the van. Mallory was with her, though."

"Have you heard anything from them?" I ask. It is much easier to talk about other people's trauma, even though I realize on some level that it is connected to mine.

"You can't have your phone on in the hospital," she tells me. "And I've only left to go to the bathroom."

"You're the best, ever," I tell her. I don't tell her that enough.

"I know," she says in her smug voice. Her smile doesn't reach her eyes, though.

There's another knock, and then a candy striper comes in with our lunch. Technically, they should only be feeding me, but part of the way the hospital staff is showing how bad they feel for me is by feeding Polly too.

"You slept through breakfast," she says, setting down the trays. They smell unappetizing, and yet I am weirdly hungry. "So I came here first when the lunches were ready."

"Thank you," I tell her. I don't know her name, even though she brought food yesterday too. She's not wearing a name tag, and she doesn't introduce herself, just leaves us to our food.

Polly takes the cover off her tray and grimaces.

"And we thought camp food was bad!" I say. She hands me the button that will put my bed up into sitting position. I can get out of bed whenever I want to, and I realize that I have to go to the bathroom. They've changed my sheets twice, but there's still blood on the padding when I get up. Polly doesn't even hesitate before picking it up, rolling it into a ball, and replacing it while I head for the washroom. It makes me teary again, and I promise myself that I will spend the rest of my life making this up to her. I am careful in the bathroom, determined not to fall or have a breakdown. What I really want is a shower and real clothes, but that will have to wait.

"Do you think it's weird that I can laugh and joke?" I ask when I come back into the main room. I assume there is a lot of therapy in my future, but I'd like to have some things sorted out before I start.

"No," she says. "It's how people cope. I mean, I don't think you should do it forever, but it's okay for now."

The only gynecologist at Parry Sound Regional Hospital is male. I was unconscious the first time he examined me, and since then the hospital has been scrupulous in ensuring that the only people who come through my door are female. When he comes into my room, it is distressing how relieved we all are when I fail to completely panic.

"Hermione," he says. "I'm Dr. Shark. How are you feeling?"

I haven't had time to get sick of people asking me that yet. I imagine I will. Fortunately, I know that when he asks, he means medically and not emotionally.

"I'm still bleeding, but the cramps have stopped," I say.

"Good, good." He nods. "Are you up to talking about a pregnancy test?"

I am really glad that Officer Plummer reminded me of it first. I can think of it as being legal, not personal, and that helps me cope.

"Yes," I say. "I mean, I'll do my best."

"You are doing very well." I wonder if he says this just because I'm not screaming and crying and climbing the walls. He clears his throat. "Emergency contraceptives only prevent pregnancy if fertilization has not already occurred, do you understand that?"

"Yes." Now it's my turn to nod. "It means that if I was already pregnant, I'd stay pregnant."

"Yes," he continues. "So there is a possibility that conception already took place before you could take the medication, in which case a pregnancy test would be positive."

"When can I take the test?" I ask.

"I would recommend waiting six to seven days," he says. "Two weeks, for the best chance at accurate results.

I deflate a little bit, but I don't think he notices. Two whole weeks. It seems like hell. But there is no way I am taking a test that might be wrong. I only want to do this once.

"I have to start school on Tuesday," I tell him. Maybe my parents will let me skip.

"I would recommend taking this week off," he says. "From school and from other activities."

Thank goodness for small mercies. The doctor continues with a bunch of questions about my regular doctor and transferring records and consent forms, and I answer like he's a waiter and I'm picking between fries or a side salad. You say the stupidest things when doctors tell you that you might be pregnant without your consent or memory of how it happened. Polly never lets go of my hand.

"I've also submitted your recommendation for psychiatric evaluation." He manages to say that gently, which probably takes years of practice. Maybe he was taught how in med school.

"Okay," I say. "That's good to know."

For the first time, he is awkward. Parry Sound is not a large place. Like Officer Plummer, he is probably not used to this. When professionalism ends, he can't stop seeing me as this tiny girl, this victim of terrible things. I want so hard to prove him wrong, but I think I have forgotten how.

"Your name is really Shark?" I blurt, and the moment breaks.

"My whole life," he replies.

"Thank you, Doctor," Polly says, the dismissal clear and polite. I'm always impressed that she can do that to grown-ups. "We'll ring for the nurse if we have any questions."

"Someday you're going to have to teach me how to do that," I tell her after Dr. Shark leaves.

"My secrets come with me to my grave," she says. It dawns on me, for the first time, that having Polly for a best friend is about to become more important than it ever was before.

CHAPTER 9

LABOUR DAY WEEKEND MARKS THE end of summer. It's not the last time people go to their cottages before winter sets in, but it's the last time that it really feels like a holiday. When I was little, we used to drive home on Monday night after it got dark, eking as much summer out of Muskoka as we could. I would sleep in the car, and Dad would carry me inside when we got home. Mum would lay out my clothes and pack my lunch, and when I got up at seven for the first day of school, it would be almost like the whole summer was a dream. When I started cheerleading, Labour Day weekend became the bus ride home from Camp Manitouwabing, full of sunburned faces, tired shouting, and as we got back into cell coverage, frenetic texting. This year, as Caledon drives down the 400 in thick Holiday

Monday traffic, it's more like a never-ending odyssey into the unknown.

Polly sits up front. I'm still tired, so Caledon made a kind of nest for me on the bench seat in the middle of the van. I'm sitting sideways with my legs up, leaning against the window. I think it might actually be more comfortable than the hospital bed, but maybe it just smells better.

"Have you heard from your parents?" Polly asks.

I have my phone again, so they could call if they were on the ground. They should be just over Newfoundland right now, if my guess is correct.

"They called my aunt, and she texted me," I say.

I thought my phone would go nuts once service coverage was more reliable, but aside from my aunt no one has sent me any messages. There is nothing. It occurs to me they don't know what to say. Usually Leo is so good at breaking the quiet, even when I'd rather he didn't. I can't decide if I'm upset by his silence now, or relieved.

"How's your aunt?" Polly asks.

"Frantic," I tell her. "But that's hardly news."

Aunt Lina lives in Toronto and thinks that anything north of the 401 is completely uncivilized. She also doesn't own a car, which is why she didn't brave the wilds to come to Parry Sound to make sure I wasn't at the mercy of some village herbalist. In her text, she had said she'd be able to get up late Sunday, but since we had already planned to come home on Monday, I'd texted her back and told her not to worry.

What a stupid thing to say. Of course she's worried. Words

have changed since Saturday, and I am still catching up.

"Mum and Dad should be home tonight," I say. "If traffic doesn't improve, they might beat us."

"We'll make better time once we get off the highway," Caledon says. "Are you girls hungry?"

"I can wait until Superburger," says Polly hopefully.

"Superburger was my plan, but we can do whatever you like," says Caledon. One of the reasons she is such a great coach is because she insists that we eat like real people, not rabbits, and earn our body shape through hard work. She hasn't ever cut anyone for gaining weight, which I've heard happens at other schools, even if you gain the weight naturally by growing or something. When I was in grade ten, she sidelined a girl for losing ten pounds without being able to explain it, and it turned out to be an eating disorder.

There is something very comforting in thinking about Caledon and the past.

"We should talk about next week," Polly says.

"You mean the opening assemblies and stuff?" I say. It's business, but hardly as usual.

Caledon's eyes flicker in the rearview mirror. I know she's making sure I'm not about to have a panic attack. I wonder if they're all worried that the longer I go without breaking down, the more torrential the fallout will be. To be honest, I have some concerns myself. But I don't remember what happened. Unless I think about it, or someone reminds me, I have trouble remembering that I'm a victim at all. That makes it hard to act like one. I kind of don't mind, because I think the alternative would involve never leaving my bedroom ever again.

"Just pull my lifts from the routine on Monday and hold an emergency practice at lunch to tweak the routines for the rest of the week," I say. It's not the first time we've had to do something like that. People get injured at camp, sometimes.

"Okay," Caledon says. "What about after that?"

She's asking, as nicely as possible, if I am going to quit.

"Dr. Shark said a week off was all I needed," I tell her. I really, really hope that Doctor Shark is right.

"Physically," she says. She's not saying something else. I can't figure out what it is.

"Hermione," Polly says, twisting in her seat to look at me. "The only person who knows the truth about who raped you is the guy that did it."

I nod.

"That means it could have been anyone," she says. "And we have six suspects on our—"

I gag and clamp a hand over my mouth. Before I can manage a word, Caledon expertly cuts across two lanes of traffic, slows, and opens the rolling door on the right side of the van with the press of a button. I fumble with the seat belt, and then the blankets, and finally settle for just throwing myself towards the door. Polly catches me, and then I'm on my knees in the drainage ditch, heaving up my breakfast while Polly holds my hair back.

"I'm sorry," she says.

"No, you're right," I manage between heaves. "It could be any one of them."

My mouth tastes like something crawled into it and died. Caledon can't get out because of the traffic, so she tosses Polly a bottle of Gatorade. I take a swig and spit it out.

"God," I whisper, and Polly leans in. I bite my lip and don't lean back. "What if it's Leo?"

"Look at it this way." Polly is so good at being insincere. Most people never know when she is faking, pretending to feel one way and actually feeling another. But I do. "All the boys on our team are terrible bluffers. We'll know as soon as one of them touches you."

"Yeah." I am not like Polly. Everything I feel is right on my skin. "But one of them will have to touch me."

"We'll cross that bridge when we get to it." The façade shifts, just a little, but she doesn't break out of it. Not quite. "For now, let's get off the highway, back home, and through this week."

She doesn't mean "through the first week of school." She means "the time before it becomes possible to test for pregnancy." Words are changing and I am becoming an expert at translation.

"Okay," I say, and stand up. I get back into the van, clutching my Gatorade, and arrange myself in the seat. Caledon has to wait a while for a break in the traffic to get back onto the highway, but before long we are back in the fast lane, heading south.

I manage to make it to Superburger without puking again. There are about a million people there, so we eat on the grass, on one of the blankets from my nest, and it's almost like it's a real holiday weekend. But there's a spot of blood on my skirt when I go to the bathroom, and Polly has to riffle through my suitcase to get a change. I'm catching up, remembering how I should act even though I can't remember why. By the time we leave, I can feel the fear creeping in, sliding over the sunny grass and echoing in the shrieks of the children who run around in the parking lot, making the most of that last bit of summer freedom. Once I'm back in the van, closed in and surrounded by people I trust, I feel like I can breathe again.

This does not bode well.

We pull into Palermo just after five o'clock. Caledon stops to pick up Florry on our way into town. She'd been staying with Mallory's family, and they live on a farm outside of town. It wouldn't make sense for Caledon to drive all the way back after dropping us off.

Florry throws herself at me as soon as the van door opens. I realize that I have no idea what they've told her, what they've told *anyone*. Caledon usually plays it straight, but Florry is ten, and I'm not sure I want to be the one who tells her what happened. Polly and Caledon both watch me while Florry hugs me to death, and once again I do not break down. I mentally check off getting hugged by a ten-year-old girl as something I can still do.

Mallory is standing outside the van, staring at me. I can tell she feels the same guilt as Polly, except worse since she was my cabin mate and because she and Polly are strong in different ways.

"Hi," I say. "Don't you dare apologize to me."

Mallory swallows, clearly on the edge of tears, and nods. "I'm glad you're okay," she says. "I hope I see you soon. At school, I mean. I'll get your homework, if you like."

That's Mallory. I should have been a better friend to her. Like Polly, she would walk through fire for a teammate. Unlike Polly, she'd be terrified the whole time.

"Thank you," I say. "I'd appreciate that. It's only for the first week."

Florry does up her seat belt, and Mallory closes the door. She stands in the driveway, waving, until we turn at the end of the laneway.

"You're not going to quit, are you?" asks Florry as we turn back onto the main road. "On the bus on the way home, Jenny said you'd quit."

"I'm not going to quit, Florry." I look up and see that Polly has turned around again, and that Caledon is looking at me in the mirror. "I am not going to quit."

CHAPTER 10

IT TAKES POLLY ABOUT FIFTEEN MINUTES to convince Caledon that we'll be okay if she leaves us at my house until my parents get home. There's a message on the answering machine that says they're leaving the airport. Even with traffic, they should still be home in about an hour. I can last an hour in my own house.

"Florry has school tomorrow too," Polly says, in a final effort to convince Caledon that other people need her more than I do.

"We'll be fine," I promise.

Caledon isn't completely thrilled, but she does nod. "Come on, Florry," she says. "We have to get you organized for the morning."

I fight down a wave of guilt. Caledon expected to have Sunday and the holiday to get herself and her daughter ready for the new school year. Now it's after dinner on Monday.

"Good night, Hermione!" Florry says. She's the only one who is acting like nothing is wrong, and I kind of want to keep her around forever. But she does have to sleep sometime and, frankly, so do I.

"Good night," I say. "And thanks for driving us, Caledon."

It's automatic, and we all know it. There weren't really a lot of options. What I mean, of course, is "thank you for not making me face the bus or ride in a squad car." But it sounds much more normal.

"See you tomorrow, Polly," she says. "Hermione, call me anytime. Anytime at all, you hear?"

"Check," I say. I add her to my list of people I will, undoubtedly, take huge advantage of in the coming days. It would make me feel bad if it didn't make me feel so pathetically grateful.

And then it's just Polly and me, staring at each other in the kitchen. She's been to my house about a million times, and she's acting like she has no idea what to do.

"So," I say, reaching for something, anything. "Ice cream?"

"Sounds good." She tries to say it like she's said it a million times before, but she doesn't make it. Now that we're alone, the façade is shifting even further.

"I'm going to the bathroom," I say. "I'll meet you in the living room."

I go into the half-bath downstairs and sit on the toilet seat, head between my knees. I stare at the tile floor I know like the back of my hand, tracing lines to infinity, and force myself to breathe. It's just my house. I've lived here my whole life. If I can't be here, where the hell else am I supposed to go?

Coming home from camp is usually a bit weird. It's exiting a made-up realm of bells and organized meals and situational friendships. Some bells stay, some meals are still planned, and some friendships last, but mostly it's coming home to find that nothing has changed, and that you haven't changed as much as you thought you did. This year is not like that. This year, I am missing twelve hours of my life. I am more changed than I can tell.

But I can breathe again, so I flush the toilet and pretend to wash my hands. I go out and find that Polly has put all the pillows on the floor so we can stretch out, and that she has emptied the fridge of anything that could conceivably contribute to an ice-cream sundae.

"You are taking this very seriously," I tell her.

"I always take ice cream seriously," she says, even though we both know that's not what we're talking about. This has to stop. I need the pain, though. At least, I think I might. Because right now there's nothing. And now that I've had a couple of days to think about it, that nothing is starting to freak me out.

I focus on squeezing as much ice cream into the bowl as possible. The trick is to fill it halfway, put on your toppings, and then smush more ice cream down on top. The weather is still hot, so the ice cream melts nicely under my spoon as I force it into the bowl. I decide for simplicity, and limit myself to an ungodly amount of chocolate sauce, while Polly piles on a little bit of everything. I have no idea how she is going to eat all that, but it's kind of a monument to ice-cream architecture, and I wonder where my phone ended up, because that sort of thing really should be immortalized.

"That's it?" says Polly, eyeing my sundae critically.

"Function over form," I tell her. "It's the key to any good structure."

"Whatever," she says. I watch her formulate a plan of attack and then dig in with her spoon.

"What are you wearing tomorrow?" I ask, because I think it's the question I would have asked if this were a normal year.

"Seriously?"

"Humour me," I say.

"I'm wearing my cheerleading uniform, idiot. Like every other first day of school ever."

Right. I forgot. Polly is the one who won't talk in a circle around me.

"Do you think I should quit?" I ask.

"Hell no," she says. "I don't even think you should stay home a week from school."

"The doctor said—"

Polly cuts me off. "The doctor is not a teenaged girl who will be going back to a school full of teenagers," she says. "The doctor was probably also a nerd in high school. You are devastatingly popular, which means that everyone will be talking about you."

"I think I'll listen to the medical experts," I tell her. "At least until I can think about boys my own age without wanting to vomit."

"And I'm telling you you're wrong," she says with an intensity that might melt her ice cream.

"I really don't think—" I start, but then there are lights in the driveway. My parents are home. "I think I'd be a lot more noticeable if I'm sick at school."

Polly clearly wants to fight about this, but my parents are running for the house. I'm not even sure my dad turned off the ignition.

"Hermione?" Mum calls from the back door.

"Living room!" I shout. There is ice cream and sundae toppings everywhere, but I'm pretty sure we'll get away with it this time.

"Oh my God," my mother says, moving faster than I have ever seen her move to fly across the carpet and hug me more thoroughly than I have ever been hugged in my entire life. "Oh my God, oh my God, oh my God!"

The day I found out Clara Abbey had died, I came home from school and Mum could tell immediately that something was wrong. It was difficult for me to explain to her. I mean, I could tell her that Clara was dead and that they had rearranged the desks in the classroom. What made it hard was that I told her that I really liked the girl I was sitting beside now, that I really liked Polly. It had only been one day, and I already liked her more than I had ever liked Clara. Clara was lovely and kind and dead, and Polly was this brilliant new light in my life. Mum had hugged me, about half as hard as she's hugging me now, and told me that I would always remember Clara, but that making new friends was an important part of life.

Now, here we are again. Something awful has happened, and my mother is hugging me. Except this time I can't explain what it is that I am feeling, and I doubt that she has any motherly wisdom to offer about how I can grow and learn in this experience. Maybe that's why she's hugging me that much harder. Or maybe it's that she's relieved that my rapist didn't put me all the way in the lake so that I drowned. I suppose that would be worse. A dead daughter coming home from camp is probably worse than a broken one. Of course, if I were dead, they could just bury me, like we buried Clara Abbey, and move on. Broken is harder to deal with.

That's the first time I've thought of myself as broken. Polly won't let me, I don't think, but everyone else seems to expect it. And maybe I am. Maybe this would be easier if I acted like I am broken. Then they'll be able to fix me. You can't fix something that doesn't know it's broken.

I realize, very slowly, that my father is not hugging me. He is standing in the middle of the living room, staring at my mother and me, but not making any move to join us. At first I think he is helping Polly. It's new carpet, after all. But he's not helping Polly. He's just standing there, looking at me.

I return his stare, confused, until he looks away. And then I know. He's afraid. He's afraid that if he touches me, I'll forget that he's my dad. That he's the one who dug the pit for my trampoline and installed all the mats after all those safety reports got released. That he's the first person who ever threw me up into the air and caught me. That he's the one who taught me to drive and do a cartwheel and catch a football and stand on my head.

He's afraid that if he touches me, I'll forget that he's my dad, not my rapist.

So he doesn't hug me. He just stands there, looking at the new carpet. And finally, finally, I really start to cry.

CHAPTER 11

IT'S THE LONGEST WEEK OF my life. Every morning, I wake up at six o'clock because my body thinks I should be going to practice or going to the gym, and every morning, I try to go back to sleep until I realize that I have to go to the bathroom, and then there's no going back. The day must be faced, and I insist on doing it in clothes I would leave the house in, even though I have no intention of actually leaving the house. I leave my uniform in my closet, and miss it all day long.

Mum has taken the week off work. I don't know if it's compassionate leave or if she took more holiday time or if she just told them she wasn't coming in, and since they know what happened, they didn't try to stop her. I suspect it's the latter. Dad and I have reached a détente, that's not so much a détente as me telling him that I needed him to hug me, so now he does.

All the time. We all sit around the table at breakfast and dinner, and try to figure out how it works now. None of us are sure. It's probably the scariest part of the whole thing so far. Words have changed meaning for my parents too, but the translation seems harder for them. Their words have no emotion or too much emotion or the *wrong* emotion. Not only am I broken, I've broken my parents.

Polly comes over a lot, and we spend time in the yard because it's still warm out and winter is coming. She jumps on the trampoline, and I watch with longing as she reels off one effortless back layout after another. When I look at her, I forget that I should be afraid of six of my teammates. I forget that any one of them might be guilty. I forget that I am damaged and remember that I love to fly. Mallory comes over a lot too, but her visits are shorter. She has chores on top of her practice schedule, but she is scrupulous about keeping promises, and she promised me homework. By Wednesday, I'm starting to think that Polly was right, and staying home this week was a mistake, but I really doubt my parents would have let me out of their sight. I'm still not convinced they'll let me go to school on Monday.

They don't hover, exactly, but one or both of my parents is always there. It's just shy of being annoying. It will definitely be annoying if they try to stop me going back to school. We don't talk about therapy or my looming test. I think we're all waiting on the result before we think any further than Sunday. That works for me, but I can already tell I'm falling behind in my classes, and I don't like being this far out of it a week into school.

On Thursday, Polly has to watch her siblings, so it's just Mallory and me in the afternoon. She's very skittish when I answer the door. My mother is in the kitchen, making dinner and pretending to be normal. It's the opposite of normal, though, because we've had more home-cooked meals this week than I think I've ever had in my whole life. On top of Mum's cooking, neighbours keep bringing casseroles over. I answered the door the first time, and Mrs. MacLennan practically wet herself trying to be nice while also extracting the most amount of gossip possible from "Here is a tuna casserole" and "Thank you, did you label the dish?" After that I let Mum answer the door unless it was Polly or Mal, and the food just goes straight to the freezer. Like a wake. Like someone had died. We had the tuna casserole for dinner yesterday, and afterwards I spent fifteen minutes throwing it back up. You're not supposed to eat your own funeral food. I think it's bad karma or something. So now they just pile up because Mum refuses to throw out things that are still edible.

Anyway, Mallory is clearly upset about something. I know I have about ten seconds to decide whether I want to deal with it. I can just take the homework and shut the door, or I can invite her in. I didn't used to overthink my choices quite so much. Then someone made what I've always been told is a very important choice for me, and now I tend to overthink everything else.

"Hey, Mallory!" I say, because I really am glad to see her. I mean, I'm not thrilled about the homework, but Mallory is normal and normal is good.

Except Mallory is not any more normal than whatever my mother is cooking. I invite her in anyway.

"What is it?" I ask, once we're upstairs in my bedroom. I don't close the door. Mum and Dad don't like my door closed anymore. They worry.

"Oh," Mallory stutters. She almost never stutters anymore. "I-I just wanted to tell you—I just thought—Don't, um, don't check your Facebook, okay?"

"What?" Of all the things I was expecting, advice on social media was certainly far down the list.

"Your Facebook," she repeats, voice stronger. "Probably you should just stay off the whole internet. For a while."

"Why?" Polly and I communicate almost entirely by text or phone, and I don't really live and die by Facebook. Still, at that exact moment, I want to go online more than I've ever wanted anything. Mallory seems to detect her mistake.

"Oh, shit," she says. "I've just made it worse."

"Made what worse?"

"You know how—I mean, you knew there'd be rumours, right?" she asks. I nod. "Well, I did my best. Every time I heard someone, I would tell them that you didn't—that it was a *crime*."

I am constantly surprised, these days, at the creative ways by which people will avoid saying "you were raped." Everyone's broken where that word is concerned.

"Mal," I say. "Just say it."

"I told everyone about the roofies. How they work; make you sleepy and take your memory and stop you from fighting back. I told them all. But I'm not Polly. People don't listen to me."

"People listen to you," I tell her. "They just don't fear you."

"But they didn't listen to me," she says. She's nearing hysterics, and I feel oddly calm. If I ask her to stop, she will stop. I will remain unknowing, and it will kill her, but she will stop.

I don't ask her to stop.

"Mallory," I say again. "Just tell me."

"Leo told everyone you spent two weeks flirting with every boy at the camp but him," she blurts. "And Jenny said she saw a huge box of condoms in your suitcase."

It takes a moment, a moment in which I remember how everything used to make sense, and how it didn't used to take me a moment to figure things out, and then I realize what my Facebook is going to say. What *everyone* is going to say.

"Oh." My voice wasn't always this small, hurt thing. Once upon a time, it rang in the rafters. I think that story might be over though. I think it drowned in Lake Manitouwabing. "Oh no."

"I'm sorry," Mallory says again. "I did my best."

"Thank you," I say, and I find that I mean it. In my bedroom, leaning back against the headboard with my knees pulled in, it's easier to find the parts of me that used to be brave. "Thank you for trying."

Mallory is popular enough, but she is shy. She's a cheerleader because she loves to dance, and because even though she doesn't like free fall, when she's in a lift, she can hold a pose, one foot in someone else's hand, forever. And this week, she stood up for me, over and over again. And now she thinks she has failed.

"Why would Jenny lie like that?" she asks.

"She's not lying," I say, and my throat feels sick. I'm done

87

vomiting, though. I have decided. The first year at camp, when the other campers found out my name was Winters, they tried to nickname me the Ice Queen. It didn't stick, mostly because I am so darn cheerful. I think being ice, like a glacier, would be useful right now. Maybe it's time to embrace it.

"What?" Mallory demands.

"If you're nice to a boy, they think you're flirting. I let all kind of boys lift me up, throw me around and catch me for two weeks!" I tell her. My voice is harsh. Mallory hates to be a flirt. She'll probably never talk to a boy again, and it's my fault. "And Leo planted the condoms in my suitcase himself, probably on the bus ride up. I found them, and Jenny saw me before I could hide them again."

"He'll come clean, then," Mallory says. "When he hears that rumour, he'll know it was his fault, and he'll tell everyone. They'll believe him."

I started dating Leo because it was easy and because it seemed like the thing to do. He kissed me after the championships in the spring, even though we'd only come in fourth place. And he was easy on the eyes. I liked him; he was a dependable teammate, a natural leader for the other guys, but I don't think I liked him as much as he liked me. I saw the jealousy in his eyes every time another guy touched me at camp, and I did nothing to reassure him. I had fun and I never thought about his feelings, mostly because he was doing the same thing with the girls he was practicing with. He was mad enough that he ended up thrown in the lake, and still I didn't stop. I should have been a better girlfriend.

I shake my head hard at that last thought, and it feels wrong. It is wrong. I owe Leo McKenna absolutely nothing. He's the one who lost perspective, who saw me having fun and refused to join in. I did nothing wrong, and he did nothing. It's as simple as that. If he expects an apology or something like that before he comes clean about the condoms, then he can rot in hell. I did nothing wrong.

For the first time, I feel like a victim without hating myself for it. I raise my chin and look Mallory in the eye. She looks hopeful, but still scared. She's worried about me, the way everyone is. But I add her to my list anyway. I don't even feel that mercenary about it. Caledon will do grown-up things my parents can't, and Polly will kill people if I need them to die, but Mallory will be nice. I know she'll stand up for me when things get bad. And suddenly I know without a doubt that whether I check my Facebook or not, things are going to get very, very bad.

"I don't think he will," I say.

He doesn't.

CHAPTER 12

I DO NOT THROW UP on Monday morning, but it is a very near thing. Mum drops me off early, so I am sitting in the change room, in my workout uniform (which feels a little like armour), about ten minutes before any of the other girls show up. I use the time to breathe, and plan my escape routes for the day, should I need them. Polly arrives first, thank goodness, with Mallory close behind. I know they've done it on purpose, but both of them do me the courtesy of not pointing it out.

"Hey," says Carmen. She's loud and over-happy to see me. I can tell she's dying to hug me, and I kind of wish she would, because that is how Carmen normally says hello, but she doesn't. "I'm so glad you're back! We missed you last week."

Last week. At school. No mention of Manitouwabing. I put Carmen in the denialist camp. Someday I might need that.

Then there's a flood of girls and a flurry of clothes, until eleven of us are standing there, ready and staring at one another. My team, the girls I need to trust. This is when I usually say something encouraging and lead them out onto the floor, but we're still missing a person, and the words are stuck.

"Polly," I say, "take them out. I'll wait for Jenny."

Mallory shoots me a concerned look, and the other girls all look away. I still haven't been online, but they clearly have.

"Get a move on!" I say. "If Caledon catches you lagging in the changeroom, there'll be hell to pay."

That gets them moving, albeit reluctantly. I can hear them start their warm-up, and after about three minutes, when I think I've stalled about as long as I can, Jenny slinks into the change room.

"Oh," she says, and freezes when she sees me. "I thought—I thought I heard everyone go out."

"You can't avoid me forever," I tell her. I want to be hard as nails, the way Polly is when you cross her, but I forget how to stand the way she stands. So I bend. "We're teammates."

"I know," she says, knuckles whitening on the handles of her bag. "And I'm sorry. I mean, I'm really, really sorry."

"Lots of people have been avoiding me." I don't know why I say that, why I give her that out. Since my talk with Mallory, I've had a picture of how this conversation was going to go, except it's not going that way at all. It's Jenny. She's no more hard as nails than I am. I think it might be because I'm not in the mood to fight. Or maybe because I am in the mood to fight, but I plan to save it all for Leo.

"No." She looks like she might throw up. I am so tired of that look, of that feeling, but a part of me is glad that someone else feels it too. "I mean I'm sorry for gossiping like that. It was awful of me, and if you want me off the team, just say the word."

Okay, that I had not been expecting. When I fail to say anything, Jenny keeps babbling.

"It was just that I *knew* something," she says, twisting her fingers in the handle of her gym bag. "And people were interested in what I had to say. No one's ever interested in what I have to say."

Jenny's not stupid by any stretch, but she has a very uncomplicated view of life sometimes. I completely believe that she didn't realize the damage her stories would do. In her mind, she knew she was telling the truth. She never would have thought that it might come back to bite me. I can't be mad at her, and I should probably tell her that before she starts crying, because if she cries, I'm probably screwed.

"It's okay, Jen," I say. I lean forward, but don't get close enough that I could touch her. "You didn't lie and you didn't mean any harm. It'll blow over."

"I just wanted you to know that I've got your back, now," she says.

"And Polly threatened you?" I ask.

She cracks a small smile at that. "And Polly threatened me." She exhales. I can right her world. I'm not so sure about mine. "Seriously, though. All the girls are on your side. Even if that means we have to murder one of the—"

I know how that sentence ends. One of the boys. One of my

92

teammates. One of the guys who, in about ten minutes, is going to lift me above his head, put his hands on my thighs, and hold me there.

But I still don't throw up.

"Get changed," I tell her. "I don't want to go out there alone, and I'm pretty sure if you're with me, Caledon won't make you run extra laps as punishment for being tardy."

Thus absolved, Jenny changes quickly, looking as relieved to be in her uniform as I am for mine, though probably for different reasons. When Jenny is ready, we head out onto the floor, and fall in with the warm-up. Caledon raises an eyebrow at me, but says nothing when we stop with the others instead of continuing to make up for being late.

The guys are all stretching at the back, like normal, and today I fall in beside them when we stop running. Cameron and Dion are hesitant, but meet my eyes. Eric doesn't, but he never did before either. He says hello when I pass him, though, which is typical. Clarence is gay, something I'd never given a second thought before today and for which I now feel weirdly grateful. Which leaves Tig and Leo.

"Hermione!" Tig says, like I'm a long-lost relative he hasn't seen in years. His overcompensation is terrible, marred all the more by the violence of everyone's collective flinch as he babbles on. "I'm so glad to see you! Polly was completely lacking in spirit and her choreography lacks your finesse."

I can pretty much hear Polly roll her eyes at that, but I can't help the smile that breaks across my face. Tig might be an ass, but he's honest, and he's trying. When I smile at him, it's like the elephant in the room gets bored with not being discussed and leaves. Everyone turns to talking amongst themselves as they stretch. Caledon usually wouldn't tolerate that much chatter but, like Jenny's lateness, she lets it slide.

The only person who is not relaxing is Leo. His glower deepens—which is saying something, since it's probably been sinking for a solid week now. I feel my own anger rise, but I clamp down on it. This is not the place. Leo seems to agree with me, because he turns back to Tig, and the two of them exchange a flurry of whispers while they finish stretching.

"Okay, that's enough sitting around!" Caledon shouts. "Let's start with the basketball short cheers, and go from there."

We hasten into formation. There isn't a lot of room in the gym for cheerleading at basketball games, so we have to max-imize our floor space. This means simpler routines that can be done in a straight line. But basketball is perhaps Palermo Heights' worst sport (and that's saying something), so we've al-ways paid particular attention to our basketball routines. I'm not sure anyone would come to games if we didn't show up in top form.

Because of the tight quarters, our lifts have three people in-stead of five. I'm with Clarence and Dion, and we wobble a bit the first time because Dion is hesitant to commit.

"Seriously," I tell him. "That's just not going to work. I won't break. Lift me like you did at camp."

He sets his jaw, and we do it again.

"God, Dion," Clarence says, when they've got me in the air.

I think he's meant for me to not hear, but he's just too loud for me to miss it. "She's not contagious."

I laugh so hard that I topple, and then fall right on top of him. I probably sound a bit hysterical, but I'm also on the gym floor with a guy's arms wrapped around my waist and I'm not freaking out, so I count it as a win. After he realizes that I'm not going to have a fit, he starts to laugh too.

"Clarence," I tell him. "You are an asshole."

"And I know it," he says.

"You're just mad," Dion says, finally getting into the spirit of it, "because Clarence looks better in our school colours than you do."

"It's true," I say, like some tragic heroine. "It's true. I am nearly blind with jealousy."

"That's why she has trouble in the lift," Clarence whispers, this time loud enough for me to hear on purpose.

"Then we must do it again!" Dion declares, and pulls us to our feet.

Once again, Caledon has let the tomfoolery go on longer than she would have under other circumstances. I'm glad. I need this to get back into the swing of it.

"Let's do some full run-throughs," she says, once she's gone to all the groups and fine-tuned some of the positioning. She starts the count, and we move together in and out of lifts. You'd think it would feel stupid to cheer for a team that isn't there, but I actually kind of like it.

Caledon calls out one of the Sarahs. I should stop saying

that. I can actually tell them apart, because they look nothing alike, but they're both called Sarah (with an h) and they are both fliers and they're both in grade ten.

"Did either of you do anything at camp to get a nickname?" Tig says, clearly frustrated too.

But he's said the magic word, and everyone goes quiet and looks at me.

"Weren't you trying out Digger?" I say to the taller Sarah, the one who has dark hair.

"It didn't really stick," she says. "But we can go with it if you like."

This is ridiculous. I exchange a glance with Polly. Anyone else would see a blank face that is carefully neutral. I see a face that says "I've got your back, so go for it."

"Okay, everyone, that's enough," I say. "Caledon, can I have a moment?"

"Of course," she says. "Do you want me to stay or go?"

"Stay," I say.

I wait until everyone sits down in front of me. Then I feel too tall, so I sit down. I take a deep breath, and realize that I don't even feel like throwing up. This is already a good day.

"Look," I say. "We all know what happened at camp. We were all there. I understand that some of you don't know how to feel about it. I don't either, sometimes. And I honestly don't care because I am willing to work through it. But I can't work through it if the guys are afraid to lift me, and if no one ever talks about those two weeks, and if Sarah takes a nickname just to make me feel better. That would be really stupid."

They're all looking at me, except for Leo, who is looking at his shoes, and Caledon, who is looking at Leo.

"You're all wondering what you can do," I say. "I know that because that's what everyone is wondering." Leo's eyes flick up, just for a second, and there is anger in them. I stiffen, like I'm sitting with a rod down my back, but instead of a flare of rage, it's resolve I feel. "You can be my team. Remind me of why I love this sport so much. Remind me of why I love this school so much. I don't care if you don't talk to me in the halls or in the cafeteria, but in this gym, when we're in these uniforms, I need you to be my team. Can you do that?"

There are nods, and then a chorus of yesses, and then cheers. There are nineteen people in the gymnasium, and seventeen of them have just agreed to support me. I know where I stand, but when Leo gets up, it's to leave practice without being dismissed and head for the locker room without talking to me at all.

CHAPTER 13

IT'S BOTH BETTER AND WORSE than I had imagined. I mean, missing a whole week of school bites under normal circumstances. No matter how much homework you've done, you've still missed things (like, for example, the fact that there is a math test. Today. Mallory felt really bad about forgetting to mention it, but still). Missing the first week is even worse. I feel like there are already in-jokes that I'll never get. And, naturally, people are staring at me and whispering wherever I go. The teachers, who I know for a fact had an emergency staff meeting about how to deal with me before school even started, seem out of their depth. For the most part, they are content to let me sit wherever I like (Polly saved me a seat in the classes we have together, but for the others I get to sit close to the back), and don't call on me, even when I have my hand up (which was annoying in world history, because I really had to go to the bathroom).

What makes it better is that I have a wall of supporters. Polly, of course, and Mallory with her newfound courage flank me everywhere. When Jenny and Alexis pass me in the hall, they both wave and smile like it is a normal day. Astrid straightens up when I walk past, as if to say "Yes, I am a cheerleader, which is more than most mortals can dream of, and those are my captains." It's all very nice.

The boys do their best too. Tig's gift for causing awkward moments seems to have transmuted into a gift for breaking them. When I get to chemistry, my second class of the day and the first one I face without Polly, he doesn't let me hover in the doorway for long.

"Hermione!" He uses the same over-happy tone he'd used in practice this morning, but his smile is real. "We thought you'd just gone straight to college or something, grab a stool."

There's a shocked silence, and Leo's glare again, and then the classroom just rolls on. It's like some kind of miracle. Like my new state of being has given Tig the key to his purpose in life.

About fifteen minutes before chemistry is over, the phone at the front of the classroom rings, and it turns out that I am wanted in the guidance office. This, I realize, is probably not about my college prospects.

"Just take your books," the teacher says, so I pack up my desk and head downstairs.

Our guidance counsellor is a lovely woman named Mrs. Itesse. She has counselled an untold number of graduating Bears about where they should go to college, whether they should get a job straight out of high school, and whether to take a risk on the hot lunch instead of buying a sandwich at the cafeteria. She also helps out with our yearly pregnancy, arranging for the new mother to continue classes in whatever way works best for her, and in a pinch, provides grief counselling for our yearly death.

"Hermione, please come in!" she says. She is much too cheery. I feel my defenses go up, but I sit down anyway. "I'm sorry to pull you out of class when you've already missed a week, but I figured it was better to cut into chemistry than your social schedule."

You know, that was remarkably considerate of her. Entering the cafeteria alone after everyone else has already found a seat would suck.

"I wanted you to know that my door is always open, if you need me," she says. "I know it was a rough summer."

I stare at her for about five seconds, and then I start to laugh. She hasn't shut the door, which is not very professional of her, and I can imagine the secretaries sitting down the hall straining to hear every word. Still, I am laughing because I realize Mrs. Itesse has had it relatively easy with our year. No one is pregnant (that we know of), and Clara died so long ago that we're all well through the grieving process. Until a week ago, I would have assumed that Mrs. Itesse had never dealt with a rape case before, but now I know better. *"Hey, looking for something?"* I may not remember, but I *know*. There's no way I'm the only girl who only consented to taking a drink.

"Mrs. Itesse," I say, standing up and pushing the door shut myself. "If you can't say the word *rape*, or even *attack*, I don't know how much help you'll be able to give me."

"Okay, so you were raped," she says. "And that was probably really awful. And because teachers are much more perceptive than you guys think, I'm pretty well aware of what the rumour mill is saying."

"I'm kind of not," I admit. "I've been avoiding the internet. All I know is that Jenny accidentally gave the impression I may have been asking for it."

"She spent most of Friday afternoon sitting in that chair, crying her eyes out," Mrs. Itesse tells me. "If I had to give an honest opinion, I'd say she's taking it worse than you are."

"I've got Polly," I tell her. "Jenny just gets threats."

"That was the impression I got, yes," she says. "You've set it straight with her?"

"Yeah," I say. "This morning. We're good."

"What about you and Leon McKenna?" she asks.

"Well, Leo's the one that gave me the box of condoms," I say. "But he's not exactly rushing to defend my honour. I haven't spoken with him since camp."

"Now it's your turn to say it," she says gently. I wonder if this was in the manual.

"I haven't said a word to Leo, nor he to me, since the night I was raped."

"Do you want me to mediate for you?" she asks. "It's on my list of services offered."

"I'd rather try it with Polly for backup first, if that's okay with you," I say.

"If I had a friend like Polly Olivier, I'd probably have done more duelling in my youth," she says. Then her face goes still, and she stops laughing. "Have you spoken with an actual therapist yet?"

"I was going to wait," I admit. "I mean, they put in a recommendation that I get one, and I have a referral for whenever I need it, but I wanted to find out whether I was pregnant before I started. You know, so I could start with the right therapist."

"When's the test?" she asks.

"Theoretically, as soon as possible," I say. "But I want to wait until Saturday. Then it will be two weeks since I was raped, and we'll have a better chance of a dependable result."

"Waiting must suck," she says. "I mean, I know it sucks. *I* was hoping for a positive test result, of course, but it still sucked."

"Yeah, it's anxious-making," I say. "And I can't really talk about it, until I know."

"Fair enough," she says. "I think that pretty much covers what I needed from you. This was mostly a formality to make sure you weren't hanging on by a thread."

"I think it's because I don't remember," I tell her. "I mean, some things are hard, and I'm wearing about twice as many clothes as I usually would be at this time of year, but right now it's almost like it happened—like another person was raped. Polly had to tell me all the details. I think that's why I'm hanging on as well as I am."

"Well, if you start to crack, I'm here," she says. "And if you leave now, you'll get to the cafeteria line in enough time to get the hot lunch before it congeals in its own gravy."

On the other side of her door, the hall is quiet and the secretaries seem busy. I might as well have left it open. It's hard to keep most secrets in a town like Palermo; it's too small and too many people know everyone, but I've already discovered that rape is different—a word that would prefer not to be understood, much less spoken. I wonder how well I ever understood our curse.

Mrs. Itesse's timing is perfect. I get to the lineup just as the bell rings. The guy who operates the register winks at me, like he usually does, and then catches himself. He drops my change into my hand, very careful not to touch me, and it's all I can do not to yell "I'm not contagious!" like Clarence did that morning. I'm not quite that brave, though, so I just take my food and head for the table Polly and I claimed in grade nine and never relinquished. She's already there, because she packs lunch, and after a few minutes, we are joined by the others. Six of the girls on the squad are in grade twelve, and we've all sat together since grade ten, when they joined the team. The boys usually hang around stealing French fries before going out into the courtyard to play Frisbee, but today none of them show.

"This is going to get on my nerves," I say to Brenda, because she happens to be the closest. "Am I a horrible person for expecting them to treat me normally? I mean, should I be more considerate of how they're feeling?"

Polly looks at me like that's the dumbest thing she's ever heard anyone say, and as I repeat it to myself in my head, I realize that it pretty much is.

"Don't you fucking dare," she says. I don't remember Polly swearing this much, to be honest. Maybe I'm hypersensitive. "Don't you even fucking dare."

"Polly's right," Mallory says. "You don't owe them anything."

"My mother says it's a natural instinct for you to retreat, but

103

that you shouldn't, if you can manage it," says Karen. Her mother is a psychiatrist I will not be seeing, not because I don't trust her professionalism, but because I don't want my psychiatrist to be someone in whose house I've attended dozens of slumber parties.

"What Karen means," says Chelsea, "is that you should go out into the courtyard and beat the crap out of your boyfriend, and then probably dump him, and that we will all back you up."

"Oh, and Clarence is on board with that," adds Mallory. "He said we could find another guy to take Leo's spot on the team, no problem."

"Okay," I say. "Um, watch my food? Polly, I'll shriek if I need you."

It goes quiet the moment I step into the courtyard. Last year, after nationals and the whole thing with Leo started, I had eaten lunch with him and the other boys out here a few times. I didn't like Frisbee, though, so I usually got bored and wandered back inside to sit with Polly and the other girls. Leo hadn't liked that much, but school had ended pretty soon after, and it stopped being a problem, or at least a problem that I noticed. Noticing things was apparently not my strong suit.

They're playing now, or they had been before I arrived. Clarence has the Frisbee, and he worries it in his fingers as he waits. Leo's back is to me, but he has to know who it is. Everyone who can see me is looking at me like I'm a pariah. For the first time all day, I feel like one. I think that's what makes me hate him most of all.

"Hermione," he says, turning around slowly. He almost always calls me Winters. We are so, so breaking up. Now it's just a race.

"I was thinking we should break up," I say. "Because you're clearly uncomfortable in this relationship."

"At least I respected it while it lasted," he says. Clarence narrows his eyes, and even Tig looks taken aback, but no one says anything. This will be the conversation the secretaries wished they could have overheard.

"If you think I'm going to apologize for being drugged and raped, you have another thing coming," I say. I am surprised and impressed at how level I manage to keep my voice.

"Yeah," he says, and the temper he'd mostly held in check at camp burns too hot, and right at the surface of his skin. "Because up to that point, you were a freaking saint. All your mingling so you could spy, and your practiced smiles. You basically told me before we left Palermo that I didn't matter to you, but I didn't see it until it was too late."

These are the secrets a small town knows what to do with.

There are about a million things I could say to him. I could beg and plead for him to understand. I could fly into a hopeless rage. I could break into a million pieces. Each of those are valid options that everyone present would understand and, in all likelihood, support. I could also probably get away with inflicting significant bodily harm, if I choose to.

"Leo," I say, deciding on none of the above and reverting to childhood in what is not exactly my most glorious moment, "you are a bum."

I go back into the cafeteria with my head held high. Brenda changes the subject as soon as I sit down, but my food is tasteless and the whispers around me only intensify.

CHAPTER 14

I'VE KIND OF BEEN IGNORING my parents. To be fair, they've let me do it. They've let me put off following up on the psych referral. They've let me pick at my food, night after night, without a single comment. And they've let me disappear into my bedroom and stare at the ceiling for hours at a time. I know they're talking about me—they're my parents—and I'm pretty sure my dad has been watching me sleep, but aside from that, they are waiting me out. I wish they'd be my parents again and order me to do something. I haven't washed the dishes or done laundry or dusted since I got home from Parry Sound, and nothing. I guess I broke that part of them too.

On Friday at dinner, I decide that enough is enough. My schoolmates can pretend that nothing has happened, and that is useful to me. But I need my parents to do something else. Anything else. They can try to wrap me up in cotton wool, and I'll rebel. They can fight with each other, and I'll sit tearfully in the corner. I don't care. Just something.

"School is going really well," I say, stirring my soup. "I was worried I'd be behind, having missed a week, but I'm doing okay. I like my classes."

"That's good," says my father. I miss the way he used to laugh with me and ask questions about the cheerleading squad. Not every father would treat cheerleading with the respect it deserves, but my father has always treated me like the athlete I am. Until now.

"What did you end up taking?" Mum asks.

"I got all of my classes," I tell her. "History, chemistry, calculus and PE this semester, drama, English, geography and a spare after Christmas."

"I thought you were going to take two spares?" Dad says.

"I thought about it," I admit. "But the only thing I can give up is PE, and I don't want to do that."

"Well, as long as you're not overworked," Mum says.

This could be any night, any conversation we have ever had. It's about to take a turn, though.

"Can I borrow the car tomorrow?" I ask.

"Of course," says my dad at exactly the same time my mother says, "Why?"

That's fairly typical. Dad always assumes I'm up to good while Mum wants reasons. He's not just humouring me. In fact, this is the most normal he has been since the night he couldn't hug me.

"I thought I'd go to the hospital," I say. I don't mean to be flippant, but it comes out sounding absolutely awful, and they both freeze.

"Do you want us to come with you?" Mum asks, after a quick and wordless conversation with my dad.

"Do you want to come with me?" I say. I really, really doubt my father wants to come, but to be honest, at the moment he looks less freaked out than Mum does.

"Honey, you know we're here for you," my mum says. "Whatever you need."

"I really appreciate that," I say. "Um, if you both come with me, the doctor can just tell all of us at the same time, and that'll spare us from having an awkward conversation later."

Dad starts to laugh, then looks guilty and tries to stop, but he can't. He just keeps giggling, and I start laughing too. Mum is looking at the pair of us like we are insane. We probably are. I am, I know it.

"Okay," she says, shaking her head, "we'll all go together."

And that's how the three of us end up in the hospital waiting room at nine the next morning. Mum and Dad are holding hands, and I am holding my knees. Dad tries to put his arm around me when we sit down, and I do my best not to flinch away, but I am way, way too keyed up. Any minute now, the nurse will call my name, and then I will try to pee on command, and then I'll know, one way or the other.

"Hermione Winters," says the nurse. She knows. Everyone in the room knows, but at least the hospital staff is professional about it.

I stand, and follow the nurse into an examination room. Usually, she would leave me alone until the doctor arrives, but my family doctor is male, and I don't think I've been alone with a male person since I was raped. Everyone is so considerate.

"It's a really easy test," she says. "Noninvasive, you just go into the bathroom."

"Thanks," I say. I can't tell if she's glad I'm holding together so well or if she wishes I'd have a breakdown so her story would be better later.

"Hello, Hermione," says Dr. Leigh, bustling in with a clipboard. He delivered me, just down the hall from here, actually. I'm pretty sure this isn't a talk he ever planned on having with me.

"Hi, Dr. Leigh," I say. I'm using my cheerleader voice. It's not as bulletproof as Polly's, but it does well enough.

"Okay, so Samantha is going to stay right here while we talk about the test, and then you just go into the bathroom," he starts off. Professional. The medical people always go with professional. "So, this measures a hormone that will tell if you are pregnant. The urine test gets faster results, so you don't have to wait after taking the test. If it's negative, we'll do the blood test to be sure, and if it's positive, we'll set you up with the obstetrician."

"Okay," I say. Seems straightforward enough.

Samantha passes me a specimen cup, and for the first time, I notice the bulge under her scrubs. She's pregnant, just starting to show. My hand shakes, and I nearly drop the cup, but I manage to recover.

"Hermione?" Samantha sounds concerned, and when I meet her gaze, she figures out what finally shook me.

"I'm good, I'm good," I assure her. It's not her fault she's pregnant. Well, I mean, it probably is, or at least I hope it is, and also I wish I didn't instantly think the worst of almost everyone now, but the real point is that it's not her fault that I'm overreacting.

I take a deep breath and head for the bathroom. This isn't the first time I've had to pee for specimen collection. They routinely test all high school athletes for performance-enhancing drugs. This is the first time, however, that I've done it without knowing what the result is going to be. Still, it's not exactly rocket science. I try not to think about Leo and Tig teasing the girls at nationals last year about how much easier it was for them.

I pee in the cup and then secure the lid.

"Okay," says Samantha, when I pass her the sealed container. "You just go back into the exam room."

"Can you get my parents?" I ask. "For the result, I mean? I'd rather they just hear it than have to tell them in the waiting room or the car."

"Of course, honey," she says. "I—I really hope, I mean, I don't know what to say."

"It's okay," I tell her. I don't tell her that I hope she is the only pregnant woman in this room. I'm not sure if that's polite.

"You just go on in," she says, recovering.

I sit on the table, rustling the paper and swinging my legs over the edge. Mum and Dad come in, and Dad takes the chair. Mum gets right up on the table with me, and squeezes my hand so tightly it turns red. Nobody says anything for a moment, and then I can't take it anymore.

"What was it like?" I ask. I had accepted that I was going to think about which university I was going to go to and what my major would be, but that's about as far into the future as I'd looked. Children hadn't even entered my periphery. "When you found out you were having me, what was it like?"

"It was the happiest day of my life," my dad says, without a moment's hesitation. "I mean, I've had a lot of those. The day I married your mother, the day you were born, the first time you won at nationals, the time I won the bowling league. But it's on my list too."

"I was terrified," Mum admits. "I mean, I had thought we were ready, and then as soon as the doctor said the words, I thought of all the things I didn't know, and I was scared. But I saw your dad, and I knew we'd be okay."

"You understand that I don't feel any of that, right?" I say. "I mean, I'm not sure I feel anything right now."

"Sweetheart," Dad says, "if you were glad about this, we'd have made you go to the psychiatrist already."

Mum doesn't talk as much as Dad does, so sometimes it's hard to read her. I can tell she's angry now. Her eyes bulge a little, and her knuckles are white. There's a sadness to her too. It makes her fragile around the edges. I don't like it. "The only thing that's kept me from breaking heads is the part that I don't know whose head to break. I know you think that Polly is your superhero, but in this case, she's going to have to get in line."

That makes me laugh, and this time when Dad gets up to hug me, I let him.

"I hate this," he says, and he's crying. "I hate this so much."

"I do too," I say. "And I promise that after the result, I'll stop stalling. I'll see the therapist and I'll do all the workbooks and I'll do my best to be—whatever it is I am now."

"Honey," Mum says, and she's crying too. "Honey, we don't care about that. You'll heal the way you need to. We're not going to push."

"You will if I ask, though, right?" I say.

"Of course," Dad says. "Like the woman said, Polly's not your only superhero."

It would be more reassuring if the pair of them weren't tearstained messes, but it would mean a hell of a lot less.

There's a very polite knock, and then Dr. Leigh comes in. I can tell as soon as I see his face.

"I'm sorry," he says. "I'm sorry, but it's positive."

CHAPTER 15

I DON'T REMEMBER HOW WE got home. I also know that this isn't a dream I'm just going to wake up from. Mum must have helped me to the car. Dr. Leigh probably said something helpful, and I know he took blood, because I have the bruise on the inside of my elbow I always have when I give blood. Dad drove home. But I don't remember any of it. I have enough blanks in my life. I've lost enough time. I refuse to lose any more. Even for this.

They're squeezing me in with the ob-gyn on Sunday afternoon. I don't remember making the appointment, but it's written on the calendar in the kitchen, so I know it's true. They must be rushing the blood test. The ob-gyn is Short Sarah's Mother. Living in a small town was always comforting before this. Everyone knows me. They still do. I just have things I want to keep from them, and that is hard to do when you are a cheerleader and actually like being the centre of attention, most of the time. I decide right then that I am going as far afield as possible for my psychiatrist.

Mum and Dad don't say the word *options* even once. I don't call Officer Plummer. I'm not going to until the ob-gyn tells me to. On Sunday morning we pick up Polly, and Mum drives us to the hospital again. Dr. Short Sarah's Mother must be on call this weekend. That's how they were able to fit me in on such short notice. Small-town doctors have to be able to multitask. Dad is at work already when I wake up. I hope he doesn't have to do anything too focused today.

The appointment passes in a fog. I can't remember Short Sarah's Mother's name, but at least I don't call her Short Sarah's Mother. She confirms that I am pregnant, and does me the courtesy of not telling me the odds. I know them, and they are pretty steep. Mum and Polly keep offering to leave, and I keep turning them down. I get that at some point I am going to want privacy, but right now, every person in the room is a person I love (or, in the case of Short Sarah's Mother, a person I trust), and that's what makes it real.

Finally, I am back in my clothes and still feeling more naked than I ever have before, and Short Sarah's Mother turns to me with a handful of pamphlets.

"I'm getting an abortion," I say. I hadn't thought about it until right that moment, except in the theoretical sense, but I know it is the only option I will accept. I am seventeen years old and I did not choose this. The sooner I end it, the better off I will be. Maybe that is selfish, but right now I am pretty sure I have earned a bit of selfish behaviour. Polly's face is carefully neutral, and Mum just looks resolute.

"Okay," says Short Sarah's Mother without missing a beat. She drops about half the pamphlets onto the table and passes me only the relevant ones. "The closest clinic is in Waterloo, but the best ones are in Toronto. You don't need me to set it up, just the paper that says you're pregnant. Take your health card, and you're all set."

I wait for Polly to make the obvious joke about being glad we're not Conservatives, but she's not in a joking mood, and so nothing happens.

"Just out of curiosity, who knows my result?" I ask.

"Just the people in this room," she says. "Usually the lab techs would know, but there were six other tests with yours, and we numbered them to maintain your anonymity."

"Thank you," I say. I absolutely mean it. Hopefully this means there will be no rumours. Or at least not too many rumours.

"That's all from me," says Short Sarah's Mother. "You can stay in this room for as long as you need to, and then the door is at the bottom of the stairwell."

"Thank you, Doctor," Mum says. "We'll see ourselves out."

She leaves, and I turn to Polly. "Want to walk me home?" I ask.

Polly looks at Mom.

"Of course," Mum says, even though no one asked her directly. "I'll start lunch."

We head down the stairs without talking, and Mum leaves us in the parking lot. Polly and I head out, not particularly quickly. It's a nice fall day, and we're not in a hurry. We're halfway through the cemetery before I realize that we've taken the usual shortcut, and then I grab Polly's hand, and lead her off down one of the side rows, to a grave I haven't visited since sixth grade.

We couldn't bury Clara Abbey when she died, because the ground was frozen. I mean, they could have rented a backhoe for the job, but the graves in Palermo were always dug by Sal Harkney, and his machinery was strictly summer only. Clara spent the first four months of her death in the receiving vault, where she was joined by Tabitha Joiner, 87, cancer, and Joseph MacNamarra, 65, heart attack. Clara was finally buried in April, and my mother took me out of school to see it because Clara had been my friend. I missed a math test, so I didn't complain.

Clara's gravestone is white, like the really old ones at the back under the pine trees, but the writing is easier to read. It looks old and stately. Two things Clara Abbey didn't grow up enough to be. There's a new flower there, just one, nestled in the grass. I wonder who has been visiting. Her parents moved after the accident.

"Hermione," Polly says. "I'm not sure this is healthy."

"I just have to tell her," I say. I can't explain why. "She has to know."

For the first time, Polly looks at me like she thinks I'm broken. It's awful, and I want her to stop. But I also need to do this, so I turn back to the stone.

"Clara, I'm sorry I don't ever come here," I say. "I know that's stupid, because you're dead and I'm not sure why you'd care, but I haven't forgotten you. I do my best to make sure that no one forgets you."

The cemetery is very quiet. Even though more people use it for shortcuts than burials, we're alone. Just the four of us.

"That's the thing about curses," I say. "They make sure everyone remembers. You'll always be the girl that died by a drunk driver. The check mark for our graduating class. And that really sucks. You should be with us. Or we should forget you and move on. We shouldn't set you up as something that makes us special. That's not fair to anyone, even though you're dead."

Polly has realized why I came here, why I am talking to a dead person. She takes my hand.

"I'm not going to be the other check mark, Clara," I say. "I refuse. You didn't get a choice, but I do, and I'm making it. I will not be the class pregnancy. And if that ends the curse and makes everyone forget you, well, I'm not sorry about it."

Clara doesn't say anything, and I don't get struck by lightning. I figure that means we're good.

"Okay," I say, turning back to Polly. "Crazy moment over. Let's go see what's for lunch."

"I'm very proud of you," she says, and links her fingers with mine.

"Hey," I say, "if I can't justify my decision to a dead person, how the hell do you think I'm going to live with it?"

"I'm still very proud of you," she says, and we walk the rest of the way home without saying anything.

After lunch, we go up to my room and I get the phone. I'm holding Officer Plummer's card in my other hand.

"Do you want me to call?" Polly asks.

"No," I say. "I just need to think about it."

"What's to think about?" she asks.

"If I call, they're going to round up all the guys from camp and make them take a test," I say. "I mean, one of them did it, but most of them didn't. Am I being fair?"

"You listen to me." Polly puts her hands on my elbows and squeezes hard. "Nothing about this is fair. He has ruined your life. I don't care who you have to upset or inconvenience, you are doing this, and you know it is the right thing to do. Dion asked every day for a whole week when it would be time to give his sample. He just wants you to know, and know for sure, that it wasn't him. The only boy who is going to be put out by this is the bastard who did it. So you are going to make him as uncomfortable as you can."

I dial the phone. Officer Plummer picks up, and as quickly as possible, I tell her the result and my decision.

"Miss Winters, you have my well wishes, as always," she says when I'm done. "If you call me back after your appointment is booked, I will ensure that the sample is collected in such a way that the chain of evidence is airtight. If possible, I will do it myself."

"Thank you, Officer," I say. That's a long drive for her.

"In the meantime, the OPP will start working with Camp Manitouwabing and the schools involved to gather samples from the male students and coaches for comparison," she says. "If all goes well we'll have the comparison results in a couple of weeks."

"Okay," I say. And then because I can't think of anything else to say, I say it again. "Okay."

"My phone is always on me, Miss Winters," Officer Plummer reminds me. "You can call whenever you need to. I'll answer any questions you have about our protocols, and I'm also available if you need someone to talk to."

"Thank you, Officer," Polly says, taking the phone when it becomes apparent that I am completely out of things to say. "She'll call you if she needs you."

They exchange good-byes, and then Polly hangs up. She leans forward—right in my face—all teeth and ferocity, and takes me by the shoulders. "Bastard left a sample after all," she says. And then she starts to cry.

CHAPTER 16

ON MONDAY MORNING WHEN MY father drops me off before school for practice, there is an OPP car parked out front. For the first time since I made my decision, I'm a little bit scared. Everyone knows that there weren't any biological samples. It's practically the first thing Polly told me when I woke up. If all of a sudden the police announce they have something, someone is bound to do the math, and then the rumour mill will start up again. I'm not sure I can deal with that. Polly can somehow tell this as soon as she sees me. Her silent appraisal is enough to give me my spine back. I nod, and we get changed in silence.

"Come on in, everyone," Caledon says when we go out into the gym, and we sit down in front of her instead of starting our warm-up. "You all know Constable Forrest," she says, and indicates the uniformed officer. He's either on duty early or this is a special occasion.

"Good morning, guys," Forrest says casually. "I know you're all busy with practice, so I wanted to get right into it. You all know that one of your teammates was attacked and sexually assaulted a couple weeks ago at Camp Manitouwabing."

Everyone in the room, except for Polly, flinches at that. Well, it looks like I'm flinching. I'm actually startled, more than anything. No one ever comes right out and says it. It's refreshing.

"You also know," the constable continues, "that no biological samples were collected. However, I am pleased to tell you that one of our secondary samples has yielded testable results, which means we now have a comparison sample we can use to test against the perpetrator."

He looks right at the boys, all of whom are looking at their shoes. Then Dion stands up.

"What do you need?" he asks. The other boys stand beside him in varying states of discomfort. I'm a little bit proud of them.

"Just some cheek cells," Constable Forrest says. "I'd prefer if you volunteer them, but if for some reason you think you need a parent or a lawyer, you are, of course entitled to decline."

None of the boys decline. They line up, swabs are produced, and before much time has passed, Constable Forrest has a collection of sealed tubes, each with a DNA sample contained therein. I am almost positive that none of them will match. Dion and Cameron both looked relieved once their sample has been collected. Clarence hands his over, chewing on his bottom lip. Eric turns bright red. Tig and Leo are straight-faced, but I don't think it's guilt. Tig probably isn't fully awake yet, and Leo is still looking at his shoes. For the first time, I force myself to really consider that it was him. I brace for the nausea I'm sure will follow, but it doesn't come. I've known Leo for too long, kept too many of his secrets, even though I wasn't sure what I'd done to earn them in the first place. We were a series of miscommunications, but not that far. I don't know how I'm so sure—all I can remember is a boy's voice—but I know it wasn't him.

"Thank you all very much," he says, and then he heads towards the gym door. When he leaves, he walks right under the row of banners, dating to the mid-seventies, from when Palermo Heights was good at sports instead of being good at cheerleading. The banner above the middle of the doorway is senior boys' basketball, and Constable Forrest was a starting forward the year it was won. He left town, of course, for police college, but he came back. A lot of people do. I have decided that I am not going to be one of them.

"On your feet, girls," Caledon says. "Warm-up time."

We start to run. Caledon is watching me closely. I feel exactly the same as I did on Friday, the same as I did before. I don't feel like my body is doing something of evolutionary importance. But she can tell. The police officer might have been obtuse enough for the boys, but Caledon has figured it out. I hope not too many other people are as insightful as she is.

We run and stretch, and then it's all choreography until Caledon dismisses us for school. Everyone makes for the showers, but I cross the floor in the opposite direction, to where Caledon is collecting the cones we used to mark the floor for formation.

"Polly and I are going to miss practice a week from Friday," I tell her. I don't ask. Missing practice does not usually go over well with Caledon. But here we are.

"I'll work around you," she says. Yeah, she definitely knows. And she knows what I am going to do.

"After that, I should be back full-time, though," I say. I wonder whether some part of me will always try to be that healthy, well-adjusted person who got on a school bus three weeks ago. I wonder whether that's part of healing. I should definitely call that therapist as soon as possible.

"Don't push too hard," she says. I am almost positive she means the exact opposite, though.

"Can I ask a ridiculously personal question?" I ask.

"Yes," she says. The smile on her face is kind, and unlike anything I've ever seen from her before. "And no, Florry's father has never been part of her life. I knew he wasn't going to be, right from the start, and I knew what my options were. It was hard, but I did it, and I'm glad I did."

I freeze. She seems so sure. She never talks about herself, though she puts up with a tremendous amount of chatter from self-involved high school students. I know her degree is in health sciences, and I know she went to teachers' college, because she's a teacher, but aside from that, our coach is a mystery, one who's spent the better part of a decade pushing me to be what I am today.

"It's not the same." She holds the stack of cones in her hand

and leans back against the stage looking at me with a serious face. "You and I, we're not the same. Not even close. I said yes, and you didn't even get asked the question. A lot of people are going to say some truly stupid things to you in the near future, and if you happen to punch any of them in the face in front of me, I'm not going to do anything about it."

"Thanks," I say. "And I'll do my best to make sure Friday is the last practice I miss."

"Okay," she says. "Now you better book it, or I'll be writing you a late slip."

I make it to history just before the bell, and we're neck deep in whether the War of 1812 was a British victory or an unfortunate draw for the next hour. Usually I would love this back and forth. The teacher plays devil's advocate and keeps asking questions designed to side with the Americans, but her heart's not really in it, and we never get much past "if you attack and don't gain anything, you've lost."

We've got a lab day in chemistry, which I had totally forgotten about, and somehow I end up working with Tig, both of us knocking heads over the Bunsen burner while we try not to spill anything or explode.

"So, are we allowed to be friends still, or what?" I ask, when he goes more than twenty minutes without making a sarcastic comment about the fact that since I forgot it was lab day, I had to tie my hair back with string.

"You mean since I voluntarily gave the DNA sample that will clear me for sure?" he asks.

"No, God, no," I say. "I meant since your best friend and I kind of dumped each other very publicly the other day at lunch."

"Oh, that," Tig says. "Boys are a bit different from girls when it comes to that, I think."

"In that Leo's not going to break up with you if you talk with me?" I ask.

"Our relationship is very stable," he says, sounding like himself again. "We can survive a little divergence of social groups. And hey, I picked you to be my lab partner, didn't I?"

"I think that was more a case of 'both of us got here at the same time,'" I say, but I feel better anyway. Tig being an ass is one of the most important foundation pieces in my life, at least at school.

"You say tomato, I say tomato," he says, pronouncing both *a*'s the long way. "Do you want to talk about our feelings now? Because I should put down the acid if I'm going to cry."

"Don't be a jerk," I say. Except I really do want to talk about my feelings. I'm pretty sure no one will overhear us. Everyone is busy and chatting with their lab partners. Unlike grade nine chemistry, where we were packed in like sardines, this class is actually spaced out on the lab benches. As long as I keep it together, we could probably talk about anything. "Okay, be a jerk," I say. "But just tell me: Does Leo honestly think that I wasn't raped?"

"I would punch him in his face." Tig's whole body goes still when he says it, which is not usual for him, and I know that he is more serious than I have ever seen him in my entire life.

"In his face. But he does have a jealous streak, and he's kind of upset about how much time you spent with other guys those weeks. How you always seemed to make time for Polly, but not him. Like, he feels that had you been dancing with him like you were supposed to, none of this would have happened."

"Like I was *supposed to*?" I drop my voice to a whisper to avoid squeaking, and a couple students look our way. I glare, and they turn back to their own workspace.

"Calm down," Tig says, which only makes me more angry, but he's got a point. "I'm not saying he's right, and frankly I think that's kind of an assholish stance to take, but that's where his head's at, and you did ask."

I turn the gas on and light the burner. We set the beaker on the mesh to boil, and take half a step back to wait. I check the thermometer, and realize that when he got supplies Tig got one with the wrong range.

"Watch the beaker," I say, and head for the supply cabinet.

Leo is there. He must have had the same issue. He looks at me, and all the anger and helplessness I felt in the doctor's office, in the cemetery, in my bedroom, in the change room, and everywhere else I've been since I got back to Palermo bubbles over. He thinks I brought it on myself. And he thinks that's a good reason to turn on me.

He starts to look away, and I reach out to grab the cabinet door. And then, without meaning to, I slap him across the face as hard as I can, and stalk out of the room.

CHAPTER 17

THE CLINIC I'VE BOOKED MY abortion at in the hopes of avoiding local scrutiny requires me to be four weeks' pregnant when I show up for the procedure. This means I have to spend another week in purgatory, waiting for my body to catch up with the rest of the world. It's rapidly becoming my least favourite thing. Well, that and the feeling I have every morning when I wake up and remember what's happened to me in the first place.

So I start running after school. I don't wear my practice uniform or any Palermo Heights gear. And I'm glad it's cool enough now that sleeves and tights aren't unreasonable. As the four weeks wind down, I run all over Palermo's streets, but I feel like I'm running in place; waiting for my body to catch up and the light to change.

When I ask Reverend Rob not to pray for me, I'm not exactly sure what I'm doing or what I expect. It doesn't seem to faze him.

"You don't think it will help?" he asks. His tone is completely nonjudgmental. I am very impressed.

"Oh, I'm sure it does," I say in a rush. "But—and I'm not sure if this will make sense—but I can't deal with being a public figure of pity. If you ask them to pray, they'll pray, and they'll keep remembering. I'd like to be able to walk down Main Street and look people in the eye. And I don't think that's going to happen as long as they're being reminded every week."

"I understand," he says. "I did mention you in our prayer requests these past few weeks, but I'll stop." He pauses and watches me. His face is still calm. "And you had another question, yes? What's the other favour?"

"I'm hoping *you* will pray for me," I say. "I'm not sure what for. Holding it together, I guess? Or maybe falling apart at the right time?"

"I'll leave the specifics to God, and pray for your peace of mind," he says.

That seems fair. "In the interest of full disclosure, and because I don't think people should intentionally misrepresent themselves to God, I'm having an abortion." Saying it out loud gets weirdly easier and more difficult every time I do it. "If that changes anything."

He says nothing for a long time, appreciating that there's really nothing he can say. He can't say "Yes, good for you," because that's not nice. He can't say "No, don't do that," because that wouldn't be nice either. There's simply nothing *nice* about it. He hasn't stopped looking at me, though, which is more than I can say for most people. His face is empty of both judgement and pity. Lots of compassion, of course, but that I can cope with. Also, it's kind of what he gets paid for.

"It doesn't change a thing," he says.

I exhale a breath I didn't even realize I was holding. "Could you pray for my parents too?" I add. "They're also in the middle of this and not sure what to do."

"Of course," he says. "And for Polly and for the police officers who are working on your case."

"Thank you," I say.

"You're going out of town for the abortion?" he asks. He doesn't flinch or hesitate on the word.

"Yes," I say. "I mean, I could do it here. At the hospital I'd have to have my parents' permission, but they would give it. I just want to do it somewhere where I might not be so subject to rumours. I'm not ashamed, I just . . ."

"You just want your business back," he says. "As you should. It's between you and God, and whomever else you choose to be involved. My door is, at least metaphorically, always open. If someone starts throwing around stupid words like 'It's a gift,' or 'It's in God's plan,' you come right here, and I'll find you ten ways in which it isn't."

I wonder how I've known Reverend Rob all my life and never realized he was a superhero. I keep bringing out the best in people, it seems. Officer Plummer, Tig, Dion, heck, even Polly. It's very annoying. A stupid silver lining whose cloud I never wanted to see in the first place. I hope it's not supposed to make me feel better. Honestly, sometimes it's all I can do not to turn into a ball of rage about it. I liked it better when I built people up by cheering for them. That way is predictable and good exercise and fun. This way costs too much, and there's nothing in it for me. I miss the days when I was someone that people could ignore or discount, and still feel good about themselves.

"It's getting dark," the reverend says. "Your parents will be worried." He manages to say it like he would say it to any other kid out past sunset. He manages to treat me like I'm still normal. Maybe this is the way I can be normal now. I have that list of people who treat me the way I want to be treated. Maybe it's time to edit my life accordingly.

"I was out for a run," I say.

"I never would have guessed that," he says with a completely straight face, taking in my running gear and messy hair. "Do you want a ride?"

"No, I'll just run home," I say. "But maybe you could call them and tell them I'm on my way?"

"They'll probably appreciate that," he agrees, and opens his Rolodex. "Remember, Hermione, anytime. Not just Sundays at nine thirty."

"I know," I say. "And thank you, again."

I run all the way home, but for the first time since I started, it doesn't feel like I'm trying to escape something. It feels like I just love to run.

CHAPTER 18

ON THURSDAY NIGHT, I HAVE one of the worst conversations with my mother that I have ever had. I know it's coming, even though she doesn't, and somehow that makes it unfair. But as Polly says, everything about this is unfair. And I have to keep pushing.

"Mum," I say, knowing that there's no easy way to do this. "I want Polly to go with me tomorrow."

We're in the living room. I'm watching television and Mum is doing laundry. Or at least that's what it would look like if we were suddenly photographed. In reality, I am sitting on the chesterfield and staring at the wall, and Mum is folding the same pillowcase over and over again. Dad is on evenings this week. It's been quiet.

"That's fine, hon," she says. She sets the pillowcase down, finally, and starts to fold something else. "We'll pick her up on the way."

"No, Mum," I say. "Just Polly."

The laundry pile grows taller and Mum just looks at me. She doesn't understand.

"If you come . . ." This was much easier when I practiced it in my head. At least she's sitting too far away to reach out and put her hand on my knee. The distance I'm asking for starts now. "If you come, you'll hold my hand and you'll sit there and you'll love me and support me, and you'll be awesome at it. But I can't. I just can't. I'm going to need a friend. I'm going to need Polly. Because I'll need you to be my mother when I get home, and if you're there when it happens, it won't work. I need you to be my mum."

I see her parse it, what I've said, and I can imagine her telling Dad when he gets home. He'll come into their room quietly, trying not to wake her up, and she'll wake up like she always does. And then she'll tell him what I've said, and they'll both cry. In the morning, they'll act like nothing happened.

"Okay, Hermione." I can tell it kills her. It should probably kill me too, but I just can't let it. If I start, I'll never stop. "Polly can drive you."

The laundry pile keeps growing, all neat corners and flat planes, sorted into piles by owner. It would be comforting, if comfort didn't make me want to scream. I go back to watching the wall until it's late enough that I can go to bed without causing any more concern than I already cause. Then I watch the ceiling until I fall asleep.

I wake up slowly, way before my alarm goes off, which is the worst. If it's a fast snap to alertness, sitting bolt upright in bed with my fingers knuckling into the sheets, there's no way to deny what happened. A slow climb, like this morning, waking warm and cocooned in the blankets, gives me enough time to forget, and then recall; enough time for everything to come crashing back into my memory, or lack thereof, like that first time in the hospital when I made Polly tell me the details with no grace to them at all. It's not the way I like to start any day, and starting this one like that seems like a particularly bad omen. I take four deep breaths, and force myself to shrug it off. I can't eat anything, so at least I won't vomit, and I get ready for the day methodically, keeping myself at arm's length until I have made peace, again, with my life now.

Polly comes to get me very early. I have decided on a clinic in Toronto, which means we have to go early to avoid traffic. When I get in the car, Polly blares the radio so we don't have to talk. Mum stands on the front porch while we drive away. I don't look back, but I know she doesn't go inside until we turn the corner.

We drive in silence for two hours. There were other clinics, closer clinics, but I picked the one with the best reputation. Also, I picked the one that was closest to the lab where they will be testing the DNA of the fetal material they remove. Officer Plummer didn't say it was necessary, but when I told her where my appointment was, she said I had made a good choice. When we pass the airport in Mississauga, I start to navigate, giving Polly directions as she weaves in and out of traffic to get to our exit. At last, we pull into a parking lot, and Polly puts the car in park.

"Are you sure this is it?" I ask.

"Did you expect there to be a huge sign with flashing lights?" Polly asks. She looks immediately sorry. "I didn't mean it. I mean, I meant it, but I didn't mean to sound so . . . mean."

"Polly, if you were going to pick a day to be you, I would really appreciate it if you picked this one," I say. "And there is a sign. It's tiny, but it's over there."

It's small and grey, nearly blending into the side of the grey building. It says WOMEN'S HEALTH CLINIC in nonthreatening letters. There are six other cars in the parking lot, but no people around. Polly locks the car doors, and I sling my bag over my shoulder. I'm already wearing a long skirt, like it says on the website. It's the only one I own. I didn't have a top to go with it, which makes me feel uncoordinated. I don't remember why I bought it, or when, but I will never forget the day I probably ruin it. I have a change of clothes and the other supplies they suggested packed into the bag. I feel very, very small.

"Come on," Polly says, and takes my arm. We walk across the parking lot together, and Polly rings the bell.

"Name and size of party," says a female voice. She's not dispassionate, but she's not exactly reassuring either.

"Hermione Winters," says Polly. "And there's two of us."

"Come on up," says the voice, and the door buzzes open.

Inside, the clinic looks like an office building. There are grey walls with a green line painted at about waist height. We follow the signs up a flight of stairs to an open reception area. There are plants and lots of natural light. I concentrate on breathing and remembering where to put my feet. The receptionist is the woman we heard on the intercom. While she takes my information and hands me the clipboard, she buzzes two other people up.

Polly steers me into the waiting room. There are two groups there already. One is a woman who is very thin and very hungry looking. She's not really a group, because she's by herself. The clinic recommends not driving home, but the subway is close by. I wouldn't want to take transit, but maybe she doesn't have a choice. The other group is an Indian family, a very pretty girl in a perfect sari sitting between her parents. They are all very stiff in their seats. I focus on the clipboard.

At nine o'clock, when the Palermo Heights students are rising from their seats to sing the national anthem, a short nurse walks into the waiting room and calls my name.

"I love you," Polly says suddenly when I'm almost to the door.

"I know," I say.

We do our best not to snicker. That would be really inappropriate, but when I walk past the skinny woman, she is smiling.

The nurse doesn't touch me, but she takes me into a room with an oddly shaped chair and tells me what to do.

"We have to do this next part," she says. "But I'll make it fast."

"Thank you," I say, and she smiles in a way I am sure is supposed to be reassuring, but I am beyond that.

"Are you here of your own free will?" she asks.

I nod.

"You have to say it out loud," she says.

"I'm here of my own free will," I say.

"And you understand that you are choosing to terminate a pregnancy?" she says.

"I do," I say.

"You are of sound mind and have told us your complete medical history?" she asks.

"I am and I have," I say.

"Do you have any questions?" she asks.

"A police officer is supposed to get the fetal tissue after the abortion," I say. There are short cuts I could have taken, but I say the whole thing, to be sure. "Is she here?"

"Yes," the nurse says. "She's here and the doctor will collect the sample."

This nurse is probably the most tactful person I've ever met. I wonder whether she is naturally this empathic, or whether it's a learned skill. I wonder whether she goes home at night and cries, or whether she can leave all this here when she goes. She certainly knows my circumstances, but she doesn't feel patronizing at all.

"Are you ready?" she asks.

"Yes," I say. "Yes I am."

She presses a button, and the doctor comes in. The anaesthesia is explained, and the procedure is outlined one more time. I'm pretty sure I could recite it at this point. The doctor has a special collection bag. Usually, it's just a medical waste container, but this one has the OPP seal on it. My fetus might not get to be a full person, but it's sure as hell going to be official.

A blood test determines that I don't need a shot, and then they give me the laughing gas. The doctor ruled out a local anaesthetic because she was afraid I would panic at the loss of sensation. She's probably not wrong. Sleeping has been weird lately, and I've been obsessed with lost time. At least if there's laughing gas, I'll be in a good mood. As soon as I start to react to the gas, though, I do panic. The nurse takes my hand immediately, and keeps me still.

"Shhhh, sweetie," she says. "Remember, you said yes to this."

I have no idea how she knew exactly what to say to me. Maybe in addition to being the most empathic person of all time, she's also a mind reader. In any case, I'm now convinced that God put her on this earth to do exactly this job, and I hope she gets one heck of a karmic payoff for it later.

"There will be a slight cramping sensation," the doctor says, and then there is, and then it's done.

The collection bag isn't see-through, exactly, but I can tell there's a mass inside it that wasn't there before. I can't react properly to anything, though. The gas is making me fuzzy. But I remember that I picked this. That I said yes. And I don't panic or cry or anything like that.

"Okay, Hermione," says the nurse. "We just need to walk a short way to the recovery room."

I walk. Well, I shuffle. The nurse helps me change, because the gas makes it hard to do buttons and laces, and by the time I am sitting in the chair, I look like a dental patient who just had laughing gas to fix a tooth.

"I'll get you some water," the nurse says. "And then I need to go back into the waiting room. If you need me, press the bell next to your chair, okay?"

"Thank you," I say again. Then I lean forward. "Really, thank you."

"You're welcome," she says, passing me a cup, and then I'm alone.

I have just enough time to start thinking again, which would not end well, before the door opens and the skinny woman comes in. After her, about ten minutes later, is the Indian girl. Then a woman covered with tattoos. Then a woman who looks like she hasn't smiled in a decade. Then a woman. Then a woman. And we all sit there and stare at the floor.

"When I get home," says the woman with the tattoos. "I am going to have the coldest beer you can possibly imagine."

"I bought ice cream," admits the skinny woman.

"You should get Baileys," says the woman who doesn't smile.

"I asked to see it," says the Indian girl. We are all quiet. "Just to be sure. It didn't look like a person. Not even a little bit. Not like those religious people say. I did the right thing."

"Yes, honey," says the woman with tattoos. "We all did the right thing."

I've never met any of these women before, and I will never see any of them after today. I don't know their names and they don't know mine. I've been on teams and in clubs my whole life, surrounded by people who are united by a common purpose, and I have never felt anything like this. Maybe it's the gas, but until this moment, I have never felt such a kinship with a person who was not actually family. I love every person in this room, and I'm pretty sure that if they asked, I'd do anything for them.

Anything, except have a baby.

PART 3

Now is the winter of our discontent.

> **CHAPTER 19**

DR. MALCOLM HUTT DRIVES UP from London every Wednesday to meet with me in my living room. Our first meeting is the week after my abortion, the day after my follow-up appointment at the hospital. I'm healthy and not pregnant, and therefore I have decided it's time I start talking with a psychiatrist. Dr. Hutt was on the rather short list of candidates. I was not expecting him to be available so quickly, nor was I expecting house calls, but apparently he's some kind of bigwig who is nearing retirement and is looking for a challenge. That's just great. For him.

"Here's the deal," he says, balancing a travel mug of coffee on his knee as he sits on the chesterfield. His notes, or rather the blank paper that will eventually be his notes, are spread out on the coffee table in front of him. I am sitting on the love seat. It's not what I expected. "You tell me the truth, and I won't patronize you by asking dumb questions we both know the answer to, just to hear you say it out loud. Deal?"

"Is that always your opening offer?" I ask. "Or am I special?"

"You're special," he says. "I'm driving for two hours, after all, and your town appears to lack basic necessities like a Tim's."

"The coffee shop on Main Street is really good," I tell him. "And you'll only have to tell Alma your order once. She's never forgotten a thing in her life. Well, a thing that's related to coffee."

"Good to know," he says. "What are your biggest problems right at this moment?"

His question takes me off guard, and I answer without thinking. He probably does that on purpose.

"Waking up," I say.

"Because you forget what happened?" he asks.

"No," I say. "Because for a moment I don't remember where I am or what I've been doing, and it's like waking up in the hospital again."

"That makes sense," he says. "What else?"

"I'm overthinking everything," I say. "What I say, what I do. Everything. It's very annoying."

"And?"

"I'm pretty sure I'm doing this wrong," I say.

"What does that even mean?" he asks. I glare at him, and he smiles. "Seriously, Hermione. I promised no stupid questions. Just explain it to me."

"I wish I could tell you what happened," I say. "But I can't. It's not denial or willful blindness. It's not that I'm ashamed.

I'm really angry. And if I could tell you what happened, I would shout it from the rooftops."

"But you don't remember," he says.

"It's more than that," I tell him. "I don't remember what we had for dinner last Friday, but I remember eating. I don't remember asking Santa for a bicycle, but I remember getting it on Christmas morning. This—my attack—it's just this huge blank spot. I don't remember anything, and so I can't feel anything. Except, I should feel something. And I don't."

"Would it help you if I said this was acceptable?" Dr. Hutt asks. "That it's normal, even, in the face of lost time?"

"Yes," I say, after a moment's thought. It never occurred to me that I might be normal. "It helps a lot."

"Tell me what it *does* feel like, not what you *think* it should feel like," he says.

"It's a story someone told me," I say. "About a girl who went to camp and came back different. I feel bad for that girl, because something awful happened to her, but it's not empathy. Empathy means you understand someone's pain. Sympathy means you feel bad about it, and that's what I have. Sympathy for myself. This disconnect. I know it happened. I just don't remember it. Unless someone reminds me, I feel like the person who got on that bus, who went to that dance. But I don't usually remember on my own."

"Do you want to remember?" he asks.

"I don't know," I say. I drop my gaze and worry the seam on the arm of the stuffed chair I'm sitting on. "I don't know if that would make it better or worse."

"Your parents say you've been running a lot," he says. "You know that's a classic coping mechanism, right?"

"That was about the abortion," I say, looking at him again. "That I remember."

"Did you feel disconnected from the fetus?" he asks.

"Yes," I admit. "I did. But I don't think that's denial either. I didn't get morning sickness and I never felt any differently about myself, even once I knew I was pregnant."

"So to be sure I've understood you, you feel like you are not reacting properly because you don't remember what happened?" he says. "And if you don't remember how you changed, have you really changed at all?"

"Yes, exactly," I say. I can feel myself leaning forward, and pull back. It's just been a while since anyone talked to me in a way that entirely made sense. "Well, almost. There is that moment whenever I wake up. And the first day back at cheerleading, not knowing for sure if one of my own teammates had raped me, that was awkward."

"You don't think they did?" he asks.

"I've known most of them all my life," I say. "And I think I'd be able to tell if they were hiding something that big. Maybe that's the one part I am in huge denial about. The DNA test will clear them, I'm sure, but I have been coping by telling myself it couldn't have been them."

"While we're talking about your teammates," he says, "I understand that you and Leo McKenna were dating? In your questionnaire, you only said that you had broken off the relationship. Why did you?"

144

"If I have to be honest, I should tell you we kind of dumped each other," I say. "Loudly and in public. And then I kind of slapped him across the face in chemistry in what probably looked like an unprovoked attack."

"Good to know," says Dr. Hutt, and makes a note. "Why?"

"I missed the first week of school, and there was a particularly bad rumour circulated about me," I say. "Leo could have set everyone straight, but he didn't. He was jealous."

"Jealous of what?"

"My time." It sounds so stupid when I say it out loud, and yet it meant so much to Leo. "He thought I was hanging out with too many other guys at camp. He's acting like it's my fault, if not because I was asking for it, then because I wasn't with him, so he couldn't protect me. After we broke up, I found out about it, and then I just . . . slapped him across the face."

"Did you slap him really hard?" Dr. Hutt asks, showing a remarkable lack of professionalism.

"He had a red mark through lunch," I admit. It does make me smile. "But I didn't loosen his teeth or anything."

"In the long run that's probably for the best," Dr. Hutt says.

"If you don't mind me saying so, you're a very strange psychiatrist," I say.

"What, because I took the sofa and didn't ask you to pour out your life story?" he says. "That's a very old-fashioned approach."

In spite of myself, I laugh.

"It has its merits," he continues, "but you're mostly correct in your assessment of yourself. You're not acting like a person who was raped. You're acting like a person whose close friend was raped. At some point, if your memories resurface, you'll break. That doesn't make you weak. That's just how it goes. And when it happens, I will already know who you are and how you think, and therefore be in a position to help you heal."

"Thanks," I say. "I think."

"Don't get me wrong," he says. "You're a very interesting case. Most of my colleagues like to deal with flameouts because they don't require a lot of professional patience. You require me to sit here, learn as much as I can, and wait to do my job when the storm hits. I'm pretty close to retirement, so I've got time. Some other doctor, or at least some other doctor with my qualifications, wouldn't have that time, not for a fair price and certainly not in a town that doesn't have proper coffee."

"I tell you," I say again, "you are going to love Alma."

"That's beside the point," he says. "I'm going to drive here on Wednesdays, and your parents are going to come up with an excuse to leave the house, and we're going to talk for an hour. We might end up doing your calculus homework, but we'll talk. And someday it will all pay off."

"I hope so," I say. "I need calculus to get into nearly every university program I want to."

"When I asked you to be honest, I wasn't anticipating this level of sarcasm," he says. He doesn't look mad though. More that he's heard everything I could ever come up with before and has no interest in re-treading the ground. That's just too bad for him, I decide. It's my party, and I'll be overly sarcastic if I want to.

"Sorry," I say. "It's the one part of being a teenager I'm still really good at."

"Do you still go to parties and the like?" he asks.

"There hasn't really been one yet," I say. "The first few weeks are usually pretty quiet. Commencement is in a couple weeks, though, and there will be something that weekend."

He pauses, holding his mug mid-sip, and I realize he's trying to process commencement in October. I think he's also weighing whether another quaint-small-town-customs joke would be unprofessional. "Are you planning to go?" he finally asks, and I'm grateful not to have to explain. He can figure it out at Alma's.

"Probably," I say. "I mean, there's usually a cheerleading demo that night. All the graduates coming back for one last routine, and so on, and then we all go to someone's farm and everyone smuggles beer into the drive shed. If I didn't go, people will assume I'm fragile and I'm kind of over that."

"Fair enough," he says. "But you should be prepared for your memories to trigger. It could be something that makes you associate with the night of the dance at camp."

I think about the smell of pine that drove me off the country roads when I was running. It could be the smell or the dark or the pulse of the music. It could be anything.

"I don't want to be afraid," I say.

"You might have to be," he says. "But I have faith in you. You seem like the type who eats fear for breakfast."

"I'm really not," I tell him. "But I'm pretty sure my friend Polly does, so I usually lean on her."

"Find those people," he says. "I'm sure you already have, but keep doing it. People will say you're coping wrong, but really there's no wrong way. Anything that lets you keep going is the right thing, as long as it's not damaging. You need to find the way that works for you."

"You are definitely a very strange psychiatrist," I say.

"That's what makes me so good," he says. "Now, before I die from lack of culture, where on Main Street is this coffee shop you were talking about? I'd like to be home before I start dropping my *h*'s."

I give him directions (he rolls his eyes because those directions are mostly "drive down Main Street and it will be the only store that's still open"), and then show him to the door. Mum and Dad will be home in fifteen minutes, so I heat up the oven for one of the pity lasagnas we've been saving for a night when eating one won't traumatize me too badly. I think now that I have a psychiatrist, I can deal with it. If nothing else, it might give us something interesting to talk about, after we've done my calculus homework, of course. I need all the help I can get.

CHAPTER 20

I ADOPT MY NEW LIFE as normal. I weather the stares and the pity, and I do my best to shrug them off. The kids at school have stopped whispering about me, at least where I can see them, having moved on to other, more current gossip like the rumours of who exactly went naked under their robes at commencement, and what happened at the party afterwards. I can tell you that the party was pretty boring. It's been a cold October, so mostly we huddled near the fires behind the drive shed and listened to grads tell stories about university frosh week that were almost certainly not true. I don't mind though, because it finally gets everyone's attention away from me.

My teachers act like it never happened, which is fine because that's kind of how I act. Every now and then, I'll get a tiny flash—a smell or a hand on my arm—but now that Dr. Hutt has told me that I'm reacting in a semi-normal way, I stop trying to pretend otherwise. He continues to come on Wednesdays, and we do talk about my thoughts and feelings, but mostly he teaches me all the calculus shortcuts I'm apparently not supposed to learn until second year of university, which really pisses off my math teacher.

"I could profile her for you, if you like," Dr. Hutt offers, when I tell him for the fourth or fifth time that, yes, his way does make sense but I have to show my work.

"I need to be able to take her seriously," I tell him. "But maybe after exams?"

And there is cheerleading, which progresses the same way until three weeks after my abortion, when Officer Plummer drives all the way from Parry Sound to tell me the results of the DNA comparison. She knocks on the door on Friday night, the week after Thanksgiving weekend. Mum and Dad are both home from work, and I've asked Polly to come because I need her.

Officer Plummer has changed since I saw her last. When we met, she looked like a new officer, all edges and potential. I am the case that shaped her career. She had to learn new procedures and protocols to deal with me, and now she's working towards being a specialist. It sits well on her. I fight off a surge of resentment, but I'm getting used to it; that feeling of knowing you're the reason someone else has found herself, even though it's a crappy reason. It doesn't set my teeth on edge as much as it used to.

"Coffee, Officer?" my mother asks, and Officer Plummer nods. It's been a long drive, and for all I know she has to turn right around and go back when she's done talking to us.

"Hey, Hermione," she says when Mum goes into the kitchen where Dad is setting up the tray. She sounds tired. Her poker face is better, and I can't read her this time. "How is everything going?"

She's asking if school is okay. If I'm having nightmares. If I can look at boys without wanting to wrap myself up in a sheet. Her concern is genuine and professional. In that, she hasn't changed.

"I'm doing really well," I tell her. It's pretty much the truth, after all. "School is good. I don't want to hide in the bathroom every time a guy walks past me; cheerleading is going really well; and it turns out that my psychiatrist doubles as a calculus tutor."

"I'm glad to hear it," she says, and again, she is entirely genuine. I wonder whether she has come here to crush me or to make me whole.

Mum and Dad come back in with the tray and settle down on the chesterfield. They are barely holding it together. I don't know when I got to be so good at reading people. I took teenage indifference very seriously back when it was an option. Now, though, I have to consider every person: how they'll react and what they'll do. I have to have escape routes or a plan of attack. I didn't know I was capable of thinking so many thoughts at the same time. It's very annoying.

"Sorry I'm late!" shouts Polly from the back door. She hasn't knocked here since grade seven. "Mum was late home from work, and I couldn't leave Sylvia and Eddie till she got home."

"It's fine, dear," Mum says as Polly settles herself next to me in the chair. It's not really built for two people, but that doesn't usually stop us. "We're just getting started."

"I'll just get right to it," Officer Plummer says, after taking a long sip of her coffee. "The lab techs ran all the samples against the fetal DNA, and none of them were a match."

Mum makes a sound like a kicked dog and Dad puts his arm around her. I don't move, but Polly hugs me anyway.

"This could be for a couple of reasons," Plummer continues. "Fetal DNA isn't always the best source for sample comparisons. It's also possible that one of the boys who volunteered a sample somehow switched his out. All the officers were supposed to collect the samples themselves, but sometimes people aren't as professional as I wish they were."

"It has to have been someone from Camp Manitouwabing, though," Polly insists. "Can't they just test again?"

"We don't have enough of the fetal sample to run the whole thing again," Officer Plummer says. She sounds oddly heartbroken. "We have the initial results, of course, and if there was a match, that would be enough. We'd have to have a suspect." She takes another sip of her coffee. This is how she builds her nerve, I know now. "Have you remembered anything at all?" She looks at me when she says it, and I look straight back.

"No," I say. "I haven't."

"I know it's probably terrifying," she says, and for the first time, she sounds like a disinterested official, "but if you can bring yourself to relive it, it will give us our best chance to get the guy."

"It's not a matter of reliving it," I say, a bit sharply. "I feel like I never lived it in the first place. I know it happened, because there was some pretty incontrovertible proof, but it still feels like it happened to someone else most of the time."

"I'm sorry, Hermione," she says, and she's the same officer from when I woke up after the attack. "I really am. There's a procedure that I'm supposed to follow, but it always seems cold. I'll just talk to you from now on."

"I appreciate it," I say.

"There's really nothing?" Mum has recovered enough to speak. "I mean, there has to be something."

"I'm very sorry, Mrs. Winters," Officer Plummer says. "But DNA isn't the magic bullet everyone thinks it is. It's very fragile a lot of the time, and it works best in concert with witness testimony. I would suggest you consult with Hermione and her psychiatrist."

"Thank you for driving all the way down here in person," my father says. "I know it's a long way."

"It's my job, Mr. Winters," replies Plummer. "I can see myself out if you need a few moments."

"Thank you," says Mum.

The four of us sit there, staring at one another or the floor as Officer Plummer closes the door behind her. A moment later, her car starts, and then she is gone. Polly's heartbeat is steady, her chest wedged against my back in the chair. It's comfortable.

"You're very quiet, Hermione," Mum says. "How do you feel about all this?"

"I'm kind of relieved," I tell her. Polly tenses. "I mean, I want him caught and punished, but the idea of getting up on a witness stand and having to testify about something I don't remember . . . that was scary."

Dad is nodding, and behind me, Polly relaxes. She still wants to light the guy on fire, but my fear is something she can understand.

"I think," I say slowly. "I think, though, I'm going to ask Dr. Hutt if there's a more active way to work on recovering my memories. Hypnotherapy or something. If he says it's a quack, I'll let it go, but if he can help, I do trust him enough to do it. And, you guys, of course, will be there if it's too much."

"Of course, honey," Mum says. "Polly, are you staying for dinner?"

It astounds me that she can turn on a dime like that, but I suppose we both have our ways of coping.

"Yes, please," Polly says.

"Let's go upstairs until it's ready," I say, and we duck out before Dad can suggest we set the table.

"We're good, right?" I say, once we're safely in my room with the door closed. "I mean, you're not mad because I'm not mad, right?"

"Yes," she says. "I hadn't thought about the testifying part. That would suck a lot if your memory was fuzzy. Hopefully Dr. Hutt will help you recover something useful."

She's not sitting down. Usually she sits on my bed and fiddles with the pillows while we talk. I have a double, which we've shared on many occasions, whispering long into the night. Polly has always been comfortable up here, but now she's on edge and I don't know why. I don't like it.

"What is it?" I ask. "What do you need to tell me?"

"I was trying to find a good time," she says, her tone desperate. This is not the Polly I'm used to. She's unsure and nervous, and it's making me feel unsettled. "But then things kept happening."

"Just tell me," I say.

"Amy has been wanting to come and visit for a while," she says. "She wants to see you. She still feels bad about losing track of you at the dance."

"She can come and visit whenever she wants, you know that," I say.

"It's not just that," she says. "She also wants to come and visit me."

That makes no sense at all. I mean, it makes perfect sense that Amy would visit Polly. It makes no sense that Polly would feel awkward about it.

"I don't get it," I say.

"You've been off the internet for about a month now, right?" Polly says.

"Two months, counting camp, actually," I correct her. "Why?"

"Well, if you were on Facebook, Amy would have added you, and you would have seen all the conversations we've been having since camp."

"Polly, use your damn words," I say. "You are so much better at being straightforward than this!"

"We're dating," she blurts. "We've been doing the long-distance thing since camp, mostly, though I went to see her over Thanksgiving. She lives close to Nana, so I just ditched kitchen cleanup after dinner. And I didn't want you to feel like you're being passed over as a best friend, because you ARE my best friend. Amy's just . . ."

She trails off, but I'm not listening. I can only think of two things. The first is that my best friend is a lesbian and I was too self-involved to notice. The second is how I have let her touch me, all this time, when she has been keeping secrets. It's selfish. It's the worst thing I've ever done in my whole life, but I can't help it. I leave her there, standing in my room, and run into the bathroom and lock the door. And then, even though I promised myself I wouldn't, I vomit all over the floor.

CHAPTER 21

POLLY PRETTY MUCH ALWAYS HAS a hairpin, so she gets the door open in no time and finds me already cleaning up the floor.

"So, I'm good at keeping secrets, then?" she says, sitting down on the edge of the tub.

"You are," I say. "And please understand that all this isn't a reaction to you dating a girl. It's a reaction to me being kind of crazy sometimes. I have a therapist and everything."

"I'm glad to hear that," she says. "If it makes you feel any better, you're not my type."

"You have a type?" I ask, without really thinking about it.

"What, and you don't?" She laughs, and I feel like the world is spinning at the right speed again.

"I thought Leo was my type," I tell her. "Look how well that turned out."

"You and Leo always seemed . . . I don't know, *arranged*."

I snort at that, and she smiles. It's nice to know we can talk like this and I don't have to fly apart.

"All the pieces seemed to fit," I admit. "I thought we'd at least make it to the end of high school."

"Leo thought it was going to be you and him forever," Polly points out, "which was a large part of your problem."

I nod, and lean my head against her knee. We're quiet for a while and it's good.

"When did you know you were into boys?" Polly finally asks. I don't answer. Mostly because I'm still not sure. "I just assumed all the boys I knew were idiots," she tells me. "Then I met Amy."

"Have you told your parents?" I ask. This is important because my mother will have heard the ruckus I just caused, and will ask questions over dinner, and will probably call Polly's mother to congratulate her on raising a liberal, healthy, and well-adjusted daughter as soon as Polly is out the door.

"No," she says. "If I tell them before Amy comes to visit, they'll be really awkward, and I don't want that."

"Plus," I add, feeling like my old gossipy self for the first time in a while, "if you tell them, they won't let you share a room!"

Polly starts to giggle hysterically, gripping the side of the tub, and if it weren't for the smell of vomit, it would be like old times; the two of us hanging out, painting toenails or trying new hairstyles. There's a polite knock on the door.

"You two okay in there?" says my dad. I wonder whether he and Mum did paper, scissors, rock, or if he was just closer.

"I'm fine, thanks, Mr. Winters," Polly says. "Just a weird re-action to what Officer Plummer said."

"Will you be okay for dinner?" he asks.

"Oh yeah," Polly says. "I'm fine now. We're all fine. How are you?"

"Really?" I whisper.

"Hey, he had bad news too!" she whispers back. Dad can clearly hear us both, though, because he's laughing.

"We'll be ready in about fifteen minutes," he says. "I'll give a yell."

"Thanks, Dad," I reply. I dispose of the paper towels and wash my hands, splashing water on my face and gargling for good measure.

"I'm sorry I didn't tell you sooner," Polly says as we head back to my room. "The right moment never came up, and I didn't want to throw something else at you when you needed me."

"This is part of you. And I'm not annoyed or anything that you didn't tell me. I've been a pretty lousy friend lately, in terms of reciprocation."

"We're fine," Polly says as she sits down on the edge of my bed. "I just . . . I was afraid you'd be afraid of me. I know you're not afraid of the boys, not really, but you're cautious. It would kill me if you were cautious."

"I promise you can still sleep in my bed when we have sleepovers," I say, running a hand over the old comforter. "If you like, I'll even tell Amy that you don't hog the covers. Put in a good word and all that."

"Don't you dare," Polly says, turning bright red. "I haven't decided what we're doing about sleeping arrangements yet. I just don't want Mum and Dad to step in."

"I totally get that." Leo and I hadn't done much in the way of fooling around, but I was still annoyed at the shift in my parents' behaviour towards him when he went from being teammate to boyfriend. It's not like I had changed on some fundamental level. "But tell me how it goes."

Polly turns red again. I start to laugh, but I remember.

"Don't you dare," she says, perceptive as ever. "It's not the same and it doesn't count as your first time. You have to at least be conscious for it to count."

"There are rules?" I ask.

"Of course." She looks away, fiddling with one of the throw pillows on my bed. "I, um, may have looked some of them up when I was wondering if having sex with another girl would mean I wasn't a virgin anymore."

"There is nobody else like you." And thank goodness. I'm not sure I could deal with it.

We're both ensconced on the bed now, leaning back against the pillows. It's a good feeling—close and familiar. I'm kind of glad that someone in my life has made a profound discovery about herself that doesn't relate to me. That's also a good feeling after so much of the other.

"So how close are you planning to keep this?" I ask. Polly is pretty much made of Teflon popularity-wise, and I'm pretty sure no one on the team would care.

"I don't want the team to think I lied to them or something stupid like that," Polly says. My head is on her shoulder so I can't see her face. "I mean, everyone is fine with Clarence, but he's been out forever."

"Well, you know I'll take it to my grave if you like," I offer.

"Thanks," she says. "I'd like to keep it quiet to see how this thing with Amy goes. Then move on from there."

"Great," I say. "I like having a plan."

Dad hollers up from downstairs, and we go down for dinner. Polly spins the story of how she was sick with anger, and neither of my parents doubts her. My aunt calls during dinner to report that the news said the OPP were out of leads, and my mother confirms it without too many details. My aunt has been very good about watching and reading the news so we don't have to. They've kept the fact that it was fetal DNA out of the news, so even she doesn't know what the secondary sample is; only that it failed.

Mum hangs up while Polly and I clear the table. There will be more whispers at school, but after that everything will probably dry up again, unless I make a breakthrough that leads to hard evidence.

"Shit," I say, remembering my promise to Dr. Hutt. I check on my parents, who are migrating towards the living room, and then lean over to Polly. Being close to her has always been the easiest part of my life. "So, I kind of promised my psychiatrist I would tell him the truth, which means theoretically I have to tell him about you. But he's really good at the confidentiality thing. Except for the time he offered to profile Mrs. Abernathy for me, but that was mostly because he was annoyed."

"It's okay," Polly says. There is nothing insincere about her. This is the Polly I like best. "I trust your psychiatrist. I'm not sure it's relevant, but whatever."

"Well, I'm supposed to tell him if Leo starts dating again." It's not easy to talk about Leo like he doesn't mean anything, but I don't feel quite so bad when I do it anymore. "So I think it would make sense for me to tell him that my best friend is interested in girls, and is dating the girl who blames herself for not staying close to me at the dance where I was raped."

"Okay, when you put it like that, yes," Polly says. "Part of Amy's thing afterwards was that she had been watching me dance, but we've worked on that, and I think she's okay. If you're okay."

"As you are so fond of telling me, it was nobody's fault but the bastard who raped me," I remind her.

"I am very smart like that," she says, and starts to fill the sink with hot water.

When I tell Dr. Hutt, he laughs for about fifteen minutes straight, tears and everything. It's kind of annoying.

"What, did you profile that too?" I ask.

"Of course not," he says. "Teenage girls are almost impossible to pin down like that, especially when they are friends like you and Miss Olivier. I'm just laughing because it's so wonderfully real life, and I only ever get the soap opera."

"I'll do better to keep you entertained," I say. "And speaking of, we need to talk about ways for me to get my memories back."

"Because the DNA test didn't work?" he asks.

"Yes," I say. "And I thought you weren't going to ask silly questions."

"It's not a silly question," he says. "For all I know, you had suddenly been overwhelmed with some kind of morbid curiosity."

"Not exactly," I say. "And I'm not being pressured by the OPP either. Officer Plummer wants me to do it so she can catch the guy, but she's not pushing me."

"That's good to hear," he says. He settles in his chair like he's expecting to be filmed for a documentary about how annoying kids are these days. "I'll tell you something, though. I'm not a huge fan of recovering memories. Many of my colleagues swear by hypnotherapy and cognitive interviews, but I feel there is too much room for leading the patient to answers in that. If you like, I can refer you to someone, but I think I'd prefer to keep treating you, and see if we can come up with a way to get your memories back without resulting to charlatanism."

"It always works on TV," I say, as carelessly as I possibly can. I am going to find out what irritates this man if it kills me.

"Exactly," he says. "Look, you're already starting to identify your triggers. You mentioned the scent of pine from when you were running. If you can follow that, naturally and at your own pace, I think it will be better in the long run. The case is time sensitive, of course, so if you haven't recovered anything by, say, June, we'll look at other methods, but I really think this way is better."

I nod. "I'm not exactly in a rush either. Knowing has its benefits, obviously, but not knowing is also . . . good. At least for now. It's what I've learned to cope with, and I think I'm doing okay, so I don't want to change everything up."

"Works for me," he says. "And hey, you're getting an A- in calculus. Is there anything else?"

"Amy's coming this weekend," I say. "For the Halloween

dance on Friday, and then to hang out until Sunday."

"Are you worried about being a third wheel?" Dr. Hutt asks. "Like you were at the Manitouwabing dance?"

"Not like the dance, no," I say. "That doesn't really count as third wheeling. They were only just getting started. But maybe now, yes. I have no idea."

"Well, let me know how it goes," he says. "What's your costume?"

"Crap," I say, and he laughs again. I knew I had forgotten something.

CHAPTER 22

I DRESS UP AS A zombie. Polly is mortified, not because my costume is particularly scary but because I've picked the ugliest costume available. I think she's mostly annoyed that she doesn't get to do my hair.

"Seriously," she says, holding her nose while Amy sprays my wildly teased and deliberately messy hair. "Is this some weird sort of defense mechanism?"

Amy is getting used to how upfront Polly is. It's nice to see. She doesn't flinch at all, just keeps spraying. I'll probably have to avoid open flames for the next two weeks.

"No," I say. "It's what I had handy."

"At least she's not a zombie cheerleader," Amy offers.

"Thanks," I say. If there's a hierarchy to zombie costumes, I'm probably at the bottom of it. The clever and creative people go as zombie pirates or zombie nurses. I'm just a mess. It's possible that someone will think I am dressed as a homeless person.

"Are we fashionably late enough yet?" Amy asks. I think she's nervous. Her costume doesn't involve a mask, so the other cheerleaders will probably recognize her.

"We will be once I finish my makeup," I tell her.

I break out the greens and browns, and set to discolouring my face.

"Maybe you should have gone as Medusa," Polly says. "That's a hairstyle I could rock."

"Imagine how different your life would be if you could see the back of your own head," I say.

"I've given it some thought," she replies. She's dressed as the Queen of Hearts, not a princess, with an enormous crown and a ball gown recycled from some formal event her mother attended. She's added an enormous starched collar to it, and a crinoline for volume. She's striking, and every time Amy looks at her, she blushes. Fortunately the dance will be dark. And Polly will have a croquet mallet.

Amy sits patiently on the bed. Polly had nixed the cat costume she'd brought from Mississauga, and instead Amy is dressed as a vampire, the traditional sort that's all cape and fangs, not the sparkly sort that would require too much body glitter. Her hair curls much better than mine does, which mollified Polly a little bit, and is done up in a sweeping style that I fear will not survive shaking it like any kind of picture.

"Are you sure about this?" Amy asks. "I mean, you're really good under pressure, but I'm really not. What if someone finds out and it's my fault? I'm totally fine with staying in, if you'd rather."

I feel very, very intrusive, but Polly sits down beside Amy and takes her hand like they're the only two people in the room.

"I am not afraid of them," she says. It is absolutely the sweetest thing I have ever seen in my life that does not involve a puppy. "And I really want to go dancing."

"And, Hermione?" Amy says, looking up at me. "Are you okay?"

"Totally," I say. "I kind of miss dancing too, and if I do freak out, I want people I trust with me. That's Polly and you."

"Thanks," she says.

"And if someone does figure it out and starts a rumour, we'll just deal with it," Polly says. "What doesn't kill you, makes you stronger, and all that crap."

"Do you ever dream of the day when your life can no longer be adequately summarized by Kelly Clarkson songs?" I ask.

"All the time," Polly says. "Let's go. We're late enough to have missed the awkward openings. Hopefully there will be enough people now that it won't feel completely ridiculous."

It's pretty ridiculous. They have dances in the gym, because the cafeteria ceiling isn't high enough for the music rental place to hang its spotlights. The gym is way too big, both to decorate effectively and for the number of kids who show up. They do turn off the lights and let the rental company take care of everything, so at least it's not lit like a grocery store. Still, it's pretty hard to ignore the basketball nets and the tape on the floor from where Caledon has marked out our cheer routines.

In spite of that, though, we have fun. The Halloween dance usually has a pretty good turnout, because kids our age don't get too many chances to dress up otherwise. The front foyer is covered in black and orange crepe paper, and there are jack-o'-lanterns placed around the gym doors, because Mallory's dad is always happy to donate stuff like that to the school. Mallory is waiting for us in the foyer, along with Karen and Brenda. Chelsea is at her dad's for the weekend, or she'd be here too. When they see Amy, they practically mob her, shrieking hello at a pitch that has probably attracted the attention of any dog within ten kilometres, and hugging her all at the same time.

"Hey!" says Polly. "Watch the hair!"

"It's fine, it's fine," says Karen. "I didn't get this far in life not knowing how to hug someone with an updo."

Brenda links arms with me, which makes it look totally natural when Polly links arms with Amy, and we all go into the dance together. There's the typical crowd of grade tens jumping up and down in the middle of the room, and a bunch of guys hanging out around the edge of the gym, leaning against the bleachers. Caledon and a couple of other teachers patrol the floor, though I'm pretty sure Caledon is less concerned with how close people are dancing than she is with people messing up her tape marks.

Mallory totally tries to make a break for the edge, where she can watch and pretend she's counting who's here or something like that for the students' council, but Polly is ready for that, and grabs her arm.

"Oh, no you don't!" she says, shouting because of the bass.

Mallory grins, in spite of herself, and I relax completely. I'd been nervous, but this is how my life used to be, and I miss it. It's nice to be back. I let Brenda pull me out onto the floor, and the six of us dance like no one is watching.

The boys break in about four songs later, masked and hooting, and scrupulously avoiding me. Just as they settle into the circle, a slow song starts. I make a quick escape for the punch bowl, but Amy is less fortunate. Tig catches her, and she agrees to dance with him fairly quickly, with a smile on her face, even. I shoot a glance at Polly, but she's laughing too. Polly never, ever tires of getting the last laugh when it comes to dealing with Tig, and I suppose having to sit on this one for a while doesn't make it any less fulfilling.

Polly agrees to dance with Eric, who is either brave because he's masked or already drunk. I see Leo start to head towards the refreshment table too, and consider changing direction, but then Mallory surprises me by taking one for the team and grabbing his hand. He seems surprised, but dances with her anyway. There's a chasm between them, and it doesn't look like either of them are having any fun at all, but at least I can get a drink in peace. I hesitate for just a moment as I ladle myself a glass. It's not like punch bowls at high school dances don't get spiked. But Mrs. Abernathy has been camped out here since, as far as I can tell, the dawn of time, so I just have to take it on faith that she's done her job. I imagine there was a staff meeting about that too. "Hermione Winters will be at the dance," they were told, "so you make sure no one interferes with that punch bowl!" Or maybe it was more about how the teachers would like to prevent any of the students from getting drunk on school property. In any case, the punch is cold, which is what I was after, and I bring Mallory a cup as a thank-you when the song winds down, and she smiles.

The beat picks back up again, a loud and throbbing tone that unsettles my stomach and makes me feel uncomfortable. I can't place the song right away, which is unusual for me. Eric keeps us all pretty up-to-date on what's new and danceable on the music scene.

I take a sip of my drink, the plastic cup scratching against my overly made-up face, and it hits me. I drop the cup without meaning to, but there's not a lot of punch left in it, so it doesn't cause too much of a stir when it splashes on the floor. Polly, who is fake-grinding with Dion, sees me and her face clouds over. I am walking backwards, trying to get out, but there are people everywhere all of a sudden.

Tig slips in the punch and swears. He's definitely drunk, because that wouldn't usually be enough to make him fall, and he lands hard on the gym floor. There's a melee on the dance floor as Polly tries to get to me, but her skirt gets caught in Tig's arms, and there was apparently more punch than I thought there was, because all of a sudden people are sliding everywhere. My breath comes faster, and then I start to worry that it's going to stop coming at all.

Hands close around my shoulders and I start to panic. I'm about a nanosecond from screaming, when I recognize Dion. He's lifting me out of the crowd, carrying me to the edge of the gym, and when he sets me down, I've more or less got ahold of myself.

"Are you okay?" he yells. He has his face right next to my ear, and he's too close, but if he were farther away I wouldn't be able to hear him.

"It's the song," I shout back. He smells like sweat and cheap costume makeup. There's no pine. There was nothing in the punch. I'm safe.

"Hermione!" Polly crashes into me, Amy right behind her. They drag me away from Dion and towards the hallway, where it will be quieter and I can hide from the music until the song is over. It's so loud that I can't tell them that I was okay. That I felt safe with Dion. I think they needed to rescue me. So I let them.

CHAPTER 23

AMY HAS BROUGHT AN AIR mattress with her, but when we get home from the dance we scrub off our makeup and then flop on my bed like we're seven instead of seventeen. I end up between them, but when I try to move away, Polly grabs my shoulder.

"It's okay," she says. "Are you okay? You didn't say much in the foyer, and I think this is the first school dance we've ever left early."

She isn't wrong. I didn't feel like talking, because I wasn't sure what I would say, and when Amy suggested we leave, I jumped at the chance. I used to dance until they forced me out the door.

"I'm fine," I tell her. "It was just really loud and the song they played, that was the song that was playing when I drank the spiked punch at camp."

Immediately Polly is a picture of concern and Amy's eyes widen.

"Did you remember anything?" Polly asks.

"Just the song," I say. "Before then, I guess I hadn't thought about it or something, but I didn't remember what music was playing. I didn't remember the scene or anything like that. Just the song."

"Do you want to listen again and see what happens?" Amy suggested. "You could listen and we'd be here if you needed us."

It's tempting. It would mean I wasn't standing on the edge anymore. I've gone back and forth between being on the edge of the cliff and being safely ensconced in my nest so many times in the last few weeks that I'm starting to get dizzy.

"No," I say. "I think I'll wait until I have another session with Dr. Hutt. He'll know what questions to ask to help me."

Polly nods and flops back on the pillow. I wonder whether we're really going to sleep like this, packed in like sardines. "I'm starving."

"You know where the snacks are," I tell her. "I'm exhausted and I don't want to do the stairs again."

What I mean by that, naturally, is that I don't want to talk to my parents again. They were waiting for us in the kitchen when we got home, ever the competent care providers. They didn't interrogate us too badly, but I really don't want to go back down and answer more questions, inane or otherwise.

"Done and done," Polly says. "I'll tell them you are untangling that disaster you called a hairstyle. C'mon, Amy. You can carry the cups."

They head back down the stairs, already giggling again. I do my best not to think about the music or the song, or how it made me feel, and as a result I keep thinking about Dion instead. Leo and I hadn't exactly been models of teenage virtue, though we did have an unspoken agreement that one of us would keep his or her pants on. I wouldn't go so far as to say that Leo made me uncomfortable, at least not before the wild jealousy thing started at Manitouwabing, but there had always been a certain element of verboten when we were fooling around. Dion had only touched me for about ten seconds, and maybe I am only reacting like this because I was emotionally vulnerable, but he had felt so *safe*.

I wonder if he had done it on purpose. If he had somehow seen my panic, and decided to come to my rescue. He'd been dancing with Polly, after all. It was probable that she had kept an eye on me, and when she saw me start to freak out that clued him in. His costume was much less bulky than hers was, and so he had been able to cross the dance floor with greater speed. Yes, that made sense. It hadn't been anything special. It had just been very . . . nice.

I hear Polly and Amy on the stairs, and I do my best to drive those thoughts out of my head. For starters, I'm pretty sure I can never date anyone again as long as I attend Palermo Heights. The school can deal with me being a victim, but I don't think my classmates would know what to do if I started acting like a real person again, or at least the person I had been. More importantly, Dion is in grade eleven. That's just not done.

"Earth to Hermione!" Polly says, bouncing on the foot of the bed. I hear a thump and a rustle, as though half a dozen plastic bags and several bottles of pop have been deposited on the blanket. "You looked like you were about to sprain something."

"Very funny," I say, sitting up. I take a look at what they've brought back. "Good lord, did you leave anything for breakfast?"

Polly and Amy have, apparently, brought every piece of food in the kitchen and put it on the foot of my bed. My parents must be really happy that I'm having friends over again.

"Your father just kept handing me stuff," Amy says apologetically.

"It's okay," I say. "He's just glad I'm doing normal things again. I haven't exactly been a social butterfly this year, and he thinks I'm getting back to my old self. He's just overreacting a tiny bit."

"Here." Polly passes me a bag of licquorice nibs and a bottle of root beer. "And he was offering ice-cream sandwiches too, but we managed to escape before it got completely out of hand."

"Yes," I say, eyeing the chips, pop and Halloween candy that litters the foot of my bed. "Thank goodness for your speedy retreat. Thank goodness Mum gave away all the caramel apples."

"It's so cool that you guys can give away homemade candy," Amy says. "If we tried that in Mississauga, we'd probably get the police dropping by to make sure we weren't slipping in razor blades."

"Small towns have some advantages," Polly says. "Even though our nightlife is remarkably docile."

"You had a good time, though?" I ask Amy. She's probably used to dances where they play "She Thinks My Tractor's Sexy" ironically.

"Oh yeah," she says. "It was fun not to know anyone. There's all kind of expectations at St. Ignatius for the cheerleaders. You guys just blend right in."

"Well, things are a bit different this year," I say. "The team has kind of turned in on itself, in the good way, for the most part, since my attack."

"That's pretty cool," Amy says. I bristle, and she hurries to continue. "I mean, it sucks that it happened because of what happened to you, but if something like that had happened to me, well, let's just say I'd probably transfer. Or get homeschooled."

"I guess I hadn't thought of that," I say. "It was pretty bad the first couple of weeks, but it got better."

"Polly kept me in the loop," Amy says.

"Okay, before we get crazy maudlin, what the hell was up with Leo and Mallory?" Polly says. "I assume I missed something, but she practically threw herself at him!"

"We were both headed to the punch bowl at the same time," I explain. "Mallory was being a hero."

"That explains why it was the most awkward dance of all time," Polly says. "Sorry I couldn't save you from Tig, Amy."

"It was okay," she says. "He's a pretty good dancer."

"Another benefit of having a close-knit team," I say. "There's almost always a boy who doesn't mind dancing handy."

"Speaking of," Polly says. "I think I should probably warn you that Dion spent the whole time we were dancing watching you like a hawk."

"I wondered how he got to me so fast," I say. "You're usually the first one up the scaling ladder."

"So . . . ," prompts Polly. "Spill."

"Nothing to spill," I lie, hoping like hell that I am not turning a bright colour. "He took me out of the way and asked me if I was okay. Then you guys got there."

"He was awfully close to you." Amy looks speculative, but she's probably wondering if I'd been planning to kick him in the groin and run for it.

"It was really loud," I say. "I could barely hear him. I couldn't even hear you two until we got into the foyer."

Polly chooses that moment to roll on top of a bag of chips, exploding shards of baked-not-fried potatoes all over my bed. That effectively changes the subject.

"So," Amy says, when we've cleaned up most of the mess and shaken out the blanket. "Air mattress?"

"I'm tired," says Polly. "Let's just sleep here."

"Are you okay with that?" Amy asks me. I can't tell if she's worried about me being crowded or being a third wheel, which is fair, because I'm not sure either.

"If it's okay with you," I say. "But I'm sleeping on the edge, and I'm not sharing a blanket with Polly. She kicks."

"Hermione!" Polly protests. "You promised!"

"You filled my bed with inappropriate starches!" I fire back.

There's a lot of laughing as we make our final preparations for bed. Amy and Polly arrive at a wordless decision to keep their hands mostly to themselves. I realize they haven't spent a lot of the evening touching each other, and that this feel-each-other-out weekend has been entirely metaphorical. Maybe I should have insisted that they sleep at Polly's house instead of inviting them back here after the dance.

Of course, if I had done that, I'd be alone in bed with no snacks and nothing but awkward thoughts about Dion floating around in my head. I am almost pleased about it. That I can still feel this way without wanting to die or having an unfortunate flashback. If I can still feel, then maybe someday I'll be able to have sex with someone I like and it won't be a problem. But at the same time, it's Dion. He's a person, not a thing. And I'm making him into a thing with every thought, an experiment to see if I'm still a real girl.

I concentrate on an imaginary blank white wall, and force myself to breathe in and out in a measured way. Dr. Hutt suggested this if I have a panic attack, but I forgot it earlier when the music was blaring. I'm tired enough that it's relatively easy to clear my mind. I forget about Leo and Dion, about my ugly zombie costume and my fears about the punch. I make myself stop imagining what Dion will say to me when I see him on Monday morning. I make myself stop thinking about what I'll think or do or say when I see him. Beside me, Polly and Amy are whispering, very quietly, to each other. It sounds like wind through the trees. Like the waves of the lake against the rocky shore. I blot that out too. And then I fall asleep.

CHAPTER 24

WHEN I WAKE UP, I remember where I am and I don't remember what has happened. For a few glorious seconds, there is peace. Polly is on her side, hands cradling her face while she sleeps, and it is like every sleepover we've ever had. I always wake up before she does, whether we're at my house or at hers. Over Polly's shoulder, there is Amy. And then I remember everything, and the peace of morning is gone. Again.

It's snowing, so I stay burrowed under the covers with them, and wait for them to wake up. I feel like I am intruding—this should be important for them—but it's my bed, and I don't want to get up. I settle for rolling over so I'm not staring, and that's enough movement to wake Polly, who shakes Amy awake with threats of missing pancakes if she sleeps a moment longer. It's new, but my mornings of waking up with Polly were coming to an end anyway, and this is one difference in my life I can actually appreciate.

Amy drives home on Sunday afternoon, when the initial flurries have died off and hopefully after everyone will have gotten over their sudden-onset amnesia about how to drive on snowy roads. By Monday morning, the snow's all gone, but it never gets warm again.

The cheerleading team moves on to practice for the routines for the winter season, which means we focus on choreography and small lifts until it's warm and dry enough to go outside for the larger throws. It also means we start to focus on two specific routines. The first one is the routine we'll do for the alumni basketball game, which is played between Christmas and New Year's, and the second is the routine we do at elementary schools in January as part of our recruitment.

It's kind of pointless, really. Everyone has heard of us by the time they hit grade three or so, and if a grade eight student really wants on the team, they'll probably have been practicing since they were old enough to start going to Caledon's special summer camps for the elementary kids. But I like putting on a show or, at least, I did, so I don't mind. These two small routines, without huge throws and elaborate stunts, ensure that we don't focus too much on the showy parts of cheerleading. There's a lot of hard work in the fundamentals, dance, synchronicity and so on. It's not all spelling with your arms and throwing tiny blonde people up in the air.

Dr. Hutt does not understand any of this. He never fails to make some kind of insulting comment about cheerleading. Usually something like "You know, I'm impressed! I would never have expected a cheerleader to do this well in calculus." It's a bit infuriating, but nothing new, sadly. Apparently it doesn't matter how hard you work: As long as you're a cheerleader, you will never be a real athlete.

He is immediately interested when I tell him about my reaction to the song at the dance, though. We missed the first two weeks of November because of some conference he had to go to, and so it's the first time he's heard about my breakthrough. I bought the song on iTunes after the Halloween dance, though I haven't listened to it again yet. I'm not scared, exactly, but I am feeling overly cautious. Also, it's not really that great a song, which is something I'm glad of. If it was a favourite and I had to stop listening to it, I'd be pissed. When he asks, I cue the song, and then sit in my chair with my eyes closed.

"Well?" he says when it has played through once. I set it up on its own playlist, so it doesn't jump to something else when the song is done.

"Nothing," I say. "Maybe it's too quiet."

Dr. Hutt gets up and cranks the volume. He also sets it on repeat.

"Think about the dance," he says.

"Which one?" I ask.

"It doesn't matter," he says. "Just do your best to think about the noise and how dark it was and how many people were around you."

"I thought you said you didn't believe in cognitive interviews," I say, but I'm already stuck in those thoughts.

"Have you been doing background reading without any encouragement?" he asks. "Well done. Hardly typical of a cheerleader."

And another check mark for today.

"Thanks," I say.

"No more talking," he says, and presses play.

This time, I can feel the music in my bones. It's not the same level of bass, largely because my parents actually like their neighbours, but it is getting closer to the noise level at the dance. With my eyes closed, I can almost imagine I'm in the gym, surrounded by the others and dancing. The song runs its course, and I crack my eyes open when it starts again.

"Keep your eyes closed," Dr. Hutt says. Well, he nearly has to shout it.

Even over the music, I can hear the chesterfield creak. He's standing up. The urge to open my eyes is overwhelming, but I keep them shut. I feel the floorboard shift a bit under my feet, and I know that he's walking across the room to where he left his bag when he came into the living room. I can't hear what he's doing though—

I'm moving before I even think about it, backwards, over the back of the chair. Mercifully, it's heavy, so I don't tip it over. My eyes are open by the time my feet hit the floor, and I see that Dr. Hutt has a bottle of what I assume must be pine-scented furniture cleaner, though God only knows where he found it. My breath comes fast and my heart is pounding and I don't have an escape route from this room because this room is supposed to be safe, and Dr. Hutt just stands there, looking at me.

"Turn it off," I shout. I don't know if I mean the music, which is possible, or the smell, which is not. "Turn it off!"

He does, thank goodness, and once the sound is gone the smell doesn't seem so bad.

"Well?" he says, absurdly calm as he sits back down. "Anything that time?"

I come around the chair and sit down again, putting my head between my knees until my heart rate goes down.

"I think I hate you," I say.

"Even after all the calculus help I've given you?" he asks. His tone is mild and neutral, but I'm pretty sure if I tried to punch him in the face, he'd be able to stop me.

"Shut up," I say. "And no, I didn't remember anything."

"That was a pretty big reaction for someone who doesn't remember anything," he points out.

I wish I could open a window and get out of the smell, but since it has decided to be winter, I can't. "I didn't remember anything useful. Just a feeling."

"Tell me," he says. "I'll decide if it's useful."

"It's the same feeling I had at the dance," I explain. "I remember that that was the song that was playing. I remember that the air smelled like pine trees. I just don't remember anything about who I was with."

"So you're not remembering what happened, but you're starting to remember that it happened at all?" he offers, and I realize that this is exactly what I am doing.

"That's a step, right?" I say. "I mean, it's a good step."

"Yes," he says. "Assuming you wanted to remember."

"I don't, really," I say. "I mean, I can live without knowing the details, but at least this might help me with the whole afraid-of-lost-time-and-waking-up thing."

"I imagine it will," he says. "Do you want to try again?"

"No," I say. "I think that's enough for today."

"We'll just keep it for later, then," he says. Then he looks at me rather directly. "So, aside from the near flashback, how was the dance?"

"Amy and Polly seem to be working it out," I say. "Which is excellent. And Mallory took one for the team and danced with Leo so we wouldn't both end up at the punch bowl at the same time."

"Did you dance with anyone?" he asks.

"No," I say. "Well, not slow dancing. There was group dancing until the song that triggered my memory. We left after that."

"But it was fun?" he asks. "Not awkward or anything?"

"Sheesh," I say, "I didn't even get this degree of questioning from my mother."

"Your mother doesn't have extensive training in which questions to ask," Dr. Hutt points out. "Look, I realize this sounds like it's about to turn into dating advice, but the fact that you can continue to have close friendships without completely redefining them in light of what happened is a very good thing. I want to make sure you keep on this track."

"That makes two of us," I admit.

"Good," he says. "So tell me what else happened at the dance."

Dammit, how does he always know?

"When I freaked out," I say, and he grimaces, so I correct myself, "when I started to have my panic attack, one of the guys on the team, Dion, he came over to where I was. There was kind of a crowd and I couldn't get free of it, and I'd spilled my punch everywhere, and he just picked me up and carried me over to the bleachers."

"And that made you panic even more?" he asks. "Being manhandled."

"No," I say. "The opposite. It was, and I realize this sounds stupid, but it was nice. Not scary. Not exciting. Just . . . nice."

"People don't touch you very much anymore, do they? Outside of your little pep squad practices, I mean."

Two check marks. He's probably making up for the fact that he'll lose some opportunities to insult me over Christmas break.

"No," I say. I've noticed it before now, but it's the first time I've heard the thought put to words. Before I was raped, there were hands on shoulders and impromptu hugs. There was polite hassling in the hallways. Now it's only during practice, always professional, except at the dance, and look how that had ended. "I mean, Polly does, and my mum and dad have started hugging me regularly again, but not like before."

"It's likely that you miss it," Dr. Hutt says. "Even though you fear it. Both are natural. When Dion picked you up, you just had an internal fight with yourself and reason won. That is excellent news, when you think about it."

I am thinking about it, even more than I was after the dance, when I promised myself I wouldn't. Dr. Hutt is being a lot more clinical than I had been, which is both good and bad. I mean, I want my feelings to be real, but I also don't really want to have those feelings in the first place.

"Do you think I should?" I ask.

"Think about it?" he asks. "Touch people? Date again? Be more specific."

"I . . . ," I start, but then falter. I don't know.

"Look, Hermione," he says, after a sigh, "I'm really not a dating advisor. You have to make that call yourself, and then I help you with whatever fallout comes your way. I also can't tell other people how to act around you. But clearly you should think about it, because you already are. Just let me know what you decide, because I'll be able to add it to your profile."

"Are you going to write a book about me someday?" I ask suspiciously.

"Heck no," he says. "When you and I are finished, I am going fishing in the Muskokas and I am probably never coming back."

"Thanks," I say. He laughs, and I feel the need to explain. "No, really. I mean it. I'm glad that I'm not that special case that's going to make your career. I'm really sick of that."

"I know, Hermione," he says. "That's one of the reasons my rates for this job are so low."

"Any plans for Christmas?" I ask.

"Not really," he says. "Family stuff. You?"

"Cheerleading," I say. "It never stops."

"If you say so," he says. "But in any case, I'll be back in January, and you'll be able to pass your calculus finals with flying colours. Of course, that means we'll have to come up with something to talk about during your second semester."

"Don't worry," I say. "I'm taking drama. You can help me run lines or something."

For the first time, I think I've managed to unsettle him. It's totally worth it.

CHAPTER 25

IT'S FEBRUARY BEFORE I KNOW it, thanks to Christmas and final exams, both of which are so busy that everyone forgets to treat me like I am special or different or new. There's a brief moment of awkwardness at the alumni game just before New Year's when I overhear one of the former basketball players ask which one of the cheerleaders is "that raped girl." Mallory happens to be standing close enough by, and her facial expression gives me away. People stare at me for the rest of the game, but aside from that, everything is fine. We're practicing for the school tours now, and then it will be time to rev up for provincials and, if everything goes to plan, nationals.

I start to talk to my parents more, especially after I catch my dad researching e-learning programs on his laptop one evening.

"You want me to get a university degree in my bedroom?"

I snap and immediately regret my tone. I've given remarkably little thought to what my parents' ten-hour flight home from Europe must have been like, but I get an idea from my father's guilty, pained expression.

So we talk about university applications, and I explain that my goals and dreams haven't changed. We weigh distance and reputation, and pick the schools with the three best programs. I do my best to explain why I'm not a basket case. I know they appreciate it, because Dad starts being available for church on more Sundays, and Mum stops affecting a cheerfully bright smile every time she asks how my day at school was. Dad has something optimistic to pray for again, and Mum knows that I'm not just putting up a front. They didn't ask for this new daughter any more than I asked to be new, but we're making it work, and in the process we're finding out that none of the important things have changed despite all the brokenness.

I start to spend more time with Mallory and the other grade twelve cheerleaders and less time specifically with Polly. I think it's good for both of us. I know she's always going to be my best friend, and I hers, but we're going to different universities for sure, so her relationship with Amy is almost like practice for when we don't live in the same area code anymore. Amy is scrupulous about including me when she comes to town, and I've never felt awkward or like a third wheel. But I'm not there when Polly comes out to her parents. That hurts a bit, but I know what it's like to have to do something alone, so I can't really hold a grudge. She still calls me almost every night before we go to bed, and she's still the first person to rise to my defense when I need it.

We're just learning how to be ourselves in the meantime. I knew before I was raped that this year would be the end of something. I just thought I'd be able to control the ending.

I have no idea what to do about Dion. I can't avoid him because he is on the team. During practice, he is completely professional. He does the lifts and holds, and he doesn't linger. But outside of practice, I have noticed a change. He is always there, somehow, smiling and never coming close enough to touch me, but always there. I think I could deal with it if he asked me to the movies, or something. If he put his arm around my shoulder in the cafeteria. I imagine what everyone else would do. Polly might kill him on the spot. Leo would glare, but Leo always does now, whenever anyone is nice to me. Tig would laugh and say something inappropriately suggestive about cradle snatching, and Mallory would do her best to pretend like nothing was happening.

The week before the winter formal, I am putting away the mats after morning practice. I do this by myself now, because I have a spare first thing in the morning. I can shower last, even wait for the hot water to come back on, and it won't make a difference. When Dion comes over to help me, I know exactly where it's going to go, except I have no idea what I am going to do when we get there. I need to get used to that feeling now, I guess.

"Hey, Hermione," he says. At least he's calm. If he were nervous, I'd probably run away. I can handle this as long as one of us stays levelheaded about it.

"Hi, Dion." My voice doesn't crack. Excellent.

I can see him thinking, considering his options. Do we talk about hockey or the routine we just practiced? The weather?

His face shifts, and I know he's decided to dispense with all of that, and just go for it.

"Winter formal is next week. Would you like to go with me?" He says it gently, to take the edge off in case I am surprised, but I am not surprised. I still have no idea what I am going to say, though, so I pretend to be struggling with the mats. This backfires hugely, of course, because Dion is a gentleman and comes over to help.

"I'd love to," I say. I brace for the wave of panic, the lack of surety, but it doesn't come. I do want to go to the dance, after all. I have a dress and everything.

"Awesome," he says, and smiles. I see some nerves around the edges of his smile, but he's happy. I haven't just smoothed over awkwardness or avoided a scene; I have made him truly happy. I don't know the last time I've done that. "What colour is your dress?"

"Dark purple," I say quickly, thinking this will make my mother happy too. "But not quite eggplant."

He nods. He means to do this all the way. He will pick me up, and probably there will be flowers and pictures.

He still hasn't touched me. He's done all this, and he's not even sure I'll dance with him. I didn't dance with anyone at Halloween, after all, and outside of cheerleading, I haven't danced with anyone since camp.

"Okay," he says. "I'll get the tickets. Can I pick you up at eight?"

The dance starts at eight. We'll be late, and therefore not make an entrance. I'm okay with that. I let out a breath I didn't even know I had been holding and turn back to the mats. I make him happy. And he hasn't broken me. This is going to work.

Which is exactly when I know it won't. Or, at least it won't work nicely. I drop the last mat on the pile, and turn to face him.

"Dion, wait," I say.

He meets my eyes around, and I can tell he already knows. This has probably been the shortest relationship of all time. I am an awful person.

"I can't," I tell him. "I mean, I can. And I want to. But it's for all the wrong reasons. I don't want a boyfriend, and I am certainly not in a place where I can be anyone's girlfriend right now. I just—I just want—"

"You wanted to see if you can still go into a dark room with a boy," he says. "I get that. I think it's normal. Or, at least healthy."

"I don't want to use you," I say. "It wouldn't be fair."

"Thanks," he says. "For being upfront. I'm glad to know I don't scare you. That would suck."

"I'm sorry," I say. I am probably going to say it a million times.

"It's fine," he says again. "Will you dance with me, though?"

"I dance with you all the time," I joke, but it falls flat because we both know what I mean.

He is standing very close. Very close. I can feel his breath in my hair, against my ear. I am not having a panic attack. That's good. Of course, it's also exactly why I had to say no. I can't be this clinical. It's not fair. But he's not moving away.

"Just once," he whispers, and somehow it's a question. A choice I get to make. I love him, just a little bit, for giving me a choice. And that's when I realize what I'm afraid of. I'm not afraid I'll use him. I'm afraid I'll fall in love with the first person who is nice to me, just because they're nice. Thank goodness I'm not Polly's type. "Just once."

"Yes, please," I whisper back. I'm shaking. I don't want to spook him, but I can't stop. I think he's shaking too, though, because he doesn't notice.

He kisses me. Not like I'll break, but not forcefully either. His mouth is warm, and he has kissed someone else before, because he's not completely hopeless. One hand is on my hip and the other is on my neck, tangling in my ponytail. He is showered, and I still smell like practice, but apparently he doesn't care. He doesn't kiss me like I'm the girl he's trying not to scare or the girl he's trying to impress. It's just honest. Simple. Lacking in flash. Goddamn it, why must this be so nice?

When he pulls back, I'm breathing a bit harder than I should be. There wasn't a lot of heat in the kiss, and I'm not panicking, but I can feel the surge coming up behind me.

"I need you to understand," I say, holding steady. "That what is about to happen has nothing to do with you."

I really, really need him to understand. Because someday I might want him to kiss me like that again.

"I get it," he says. "Normal and healthy, remember?"

"Great," I say.

Then I turn and run into the girls' change room. Everyone else is gone, because the bell is about to ring. I get into the shower and stay there, long past the five minutes we're supposed to aim for when using the school showers. The water gets colder and colder, and I don't get out. I'm not numb. I can feel every drop of it, every icicle coming down into my hair and onto my skin. It takes away the sweat of practice, the dust from the mats, and the ache from having Polly stand on my shoulder while we practiced holds. It's not taking memories or feelings or thoughts. I am standing in the shower, and the only thing going down the drain is water.

He'd kissed me. I just stood there, but I let him kiss me. And I'm not broken. I'm not freaking out, much. I'm not crying or throwing up or using the emergency number Dr. Hutt gave me in case I have a flashback.

He'd kissed me, and I can feel the water. I feel like I am alive.

CHAPTER 26

SO, HERMIONE," ASKS THE NEWSPAPER reporter. "What has been the best thing about cheerleading at Palermo Heights?"

"My team, for sure," I say, nodding sagely like I know what I'm talking about. Every year, right before the provincial finals, there's a profile in our local newspaper about the cheerleaders, and as co-captain, I am being interviewed for it. It's a sort of bookend for the speech at the campfire, only less sincere, because the reporter has already decided what kind of story she is going to write. If we want a different one, we're going to have to work for it, and Polly and I had decided it wasn't really worth the effort. Instead, we give exactly the answers we're expected to. "A lot of cheerleading is about teamwork, literally trusting someone to be there to catch you when you're falling, and I couldn't ask for a better team than the one we've got."

Polly is doing that thing where she rolls her eyes without actually moving, and it's all I can do not to laugh. Her fake spirit is in full force, but since the reporter doesn't know her very well, she can't tell it's all a show.

"What about you, Polly?" the reporter says dutifully. "What's your favourite part?"

"Knowing that the school is right behind me, as much as I'm right behind them," Polly says. Her insincerity is excruciating, but only if you know what to look for. The reporter is eating it up.

"Good, good," the reporter murmurs to herself, writing it all down in her notebook. Then she looks up and stares straight at me. "Hermione, after your attack at the end of last summer, do you have any words of advice on how other girls can be smart, and stop such awful things happening to them?"

"Wh-what?" I stutter. Beside me, Polly's fake spirit melts into the floor. This isn't in the script.

"Maybe precautions you wish you'd taken," the reporter says. "Or something you wish you had known about before you went to Camp Manitouwabing?"

"I thought you were here to do an interview about the cheerleaders," I say, desperately stalling. I know, without a doubt, that whatever my answer is will be printed verbatim in the newspaper, and that pisses me off a bit because it has blindsided me, and I should have seen it coming. I can feel Polly start to boil over and then rein herself in. She's making me take the lead. I'll have to come up with something quickly.

"Camp Manitouwabing isn't closing down," the reporter tells me, oblivious to our sudden change in mood. "Which means that other cheerleaders from this very school will go there. Don't you think you should do your part to help prevent such a horrible thing from happening again?"

Anger has made my mind go blank. Even though I meant to say something profound and helpful, and maybe just a bit sarcastic, I instead say the very first thing that pops into my head: "If I was a boy, would you be asking me that?"

"Well, no," says the reporter. "Of course not."

"So let me get this straight," says Polly, her voice deceptively calm. "You're okay with asking a girl who was wearing a pretty dress and had nice hair, who went to the dance with her cabin mates, who drank from the same punch bowl as everyone else—you're okay with asking that girl what mistake she made, and you wouldn't think to ask a boy how *he* would avoid raping someone?"

The reporter rocks back as if Polly has struck her, and can't seem to find the right words.

"Would it be a better story if Hermione had known what she was drinking? If her skirt had been two inches shorter? If she had a lower average?" Polly is practically on fire with cold now. I've never seen a grown-up recoil like this in my life. It gives me balance, like Polly has caught me out of the air and put me on my feet again.

"Yeah, I'm not sure I want to answer the question," I say. "Since it's so underdeveloped. The only person at fault here was my rapist. Not the camp and sure as hell not me."

"I wasn't trying to imply—" she starts, desperately jotting things down in the notebook, but I cut her off.

"I don't care. Your article had better not have anything other than my quotes about cheerleading in it. I can start a letter-writing campaign like you wouldn't believe."

"And she's the nice one," Polly adds, all teeth. "We have to go to school now. Thank you for the interview."

"Good luck at the provincials," says the reporter. It's a completely mechanical farewell.

Polly takes my arm and the two of us sweep out of the gym like we own the place. And really, we kind of do. On the way out, we pass Leo, who had sat for an interview before us as the unofficial leader of the boys' half of the team. He won't meet my gaze, as always, but I know he's heard everything.

We get into the change room, and Polly starts to change into her school clothes. We were in our full uniforms today, partially for the picture and partially because it's always good to practice a few times to get to know the limitations of your skirt. I linger though. All the bruises I had are long since faded. Only the emotional damage is real, well, that and what happened when I had the abortion.

Polly is looking at me.

"I hadn't really thought about it," I say.

"What do you mean?" she asks. She pulls her shirt over her head, and goes to fix her makeup and hair.

"I know it wasn't my fault," I say. "And no one has ever suggested that it was, but that's what everyone thinks."

"I do not think that," she says. "Not even in my heart of hearts."

"You're not everyone," I say. "You're Polly. I meant everyone *else*."

"It's certainly what Leo thinks," Polly says. "And it's what television thinks. I can't watch *CSI* anymore, you know. It makes me too angry."

"Sorry," I say, grinning so she knows I don't really mean it. "I know you loved that show."

"Shut up," she says. "I'm being profound."

"I appreciate it," I tell her. "It just struck me today, is all, when she asked. I'd never heard anyone say it out loud."

"People are always going to be stupid," Polly says. "At least I think we scared her off of putting any of it in print."

"There is that," I say.

"Hurry up," she says. "I want to talk to Caledon before class starts. She was supposed to find out which designation we got for provincials."

Because Ontario is the biggest province, we are divided into two parts for the provincial level of competition. The winners of both pools plus the next highest-scoring team advance. Supposedly it's luck of the draw, but the pools always end up weighted one way or the other. If we get an easy pool, we'll be able to relax a little bit. If we get a hard pool, we might as well give up on the idea of having a social life until late spring. Caledon might never let us out of the gym.

I throw my clothes on and fix my hair. I wasn't wearing makeup, and when I turn around, Polly is standing right there with lip liner. I open my mouth a bit so she can put it on, and remember, inappropriate timing and all, about how Dion had kissed me before the winter formal.

"So, Dion kissed me before the winter formal," I say, once she's clear of my face and I'm probably not going to get a stripe painted on my cheek.

"Shut the front door!" Polly says. "You let some kid in

grade eleven kiss you? God, Hermione, where is your dignity?"

I laugh so hard I have to sit down, and when Polly drags me to my feet and out the door, she's laughing too. We're still giggling when we get to Caledon's office. Technically, she shares it with the three other phys ed teachers, but since they all teach math as well, they spend most of their time upstairs in the math department.

"I don't want to know," says Caledon, waving us in. Years of dealing with high-strung cheerleaders have given Caledon a rather blasé approach to our interpersonal shenanigans, but she looks a little more severe than usual, too severe for it to just be that we're in a hard pool. "But I did get our pool assignment."

"And?" says Polly, all business at the drop of a hat.

"Well, St. Ignatius is in the opposite pool from us," Caledon says. She has a completely straight face, and Polly, to her credit, manages to keep a straight face as well. She's not officially out at school, mostly because she doesn't care for her business to be anyone else's, but Amy has been visiting a lot, and it's not because she's part of my support group.

"That's handy," I say. "What else?"

"Our pool looks pretty good," she says. "We got both Sarnia schools, and they'll be strong, but we can take them. I'm worried about Sir Adam Beck, out of London. But I think that's it."

"Great," says Polly. "So we go to nationals. What aren't you telling us?"

I've gotten so good at reading people over the last few months that I'd forgotten how hard it is to read Caledon at all. I look at her more closely, and Polly is right. She knows something she doesn't like, and she hasn't figured out how to tell us yet.

"Usually some school in Toronto gets it, when it's in Ontario," she says. "But this year, a bunch of northern schools petitioned, and they are going to host together."

"That seems fair," Polly says. "Even if they don't qualify, they're still lots of places, and we can deal with a long bus ride if we have to go to Thunder Bay or something"

"It's not in Thunder Bay," Caledon says. "The condition was that it wouldn't be north of Sudbury, even though that rules out every place big enough to host all the people that come with a national championship."

"So, what are they doing?" I ask.

Caledon hesitates, and then leans forward.

"They've rented a space that's big enough," she says. "There will be places for people to stay and places to eat. The actual competition will be outside, which will piss off everyone from out west, but we'll be fine so I don't really care."

"Caledon," Polly says in a tone I've never heard her take with a teacher. But I've figured it out. It's exactly the kind of bureaucratic nightmare that always happens whenever northern Ontario wins the right to host anything. I put my hand on Polly's arm, because I know that when Caledon tells her, she is going to explode. Thank goodness we didn't find this out from the reporter. Polly might have blown her head off.

"They've rented the camp," Caledon says. "The nationals this year are at Camp Manitouwabing."

CHAPTER 27

I DO MY BEST NOT to think about the nationals until after we make it through the provincials. We use the same routine for both, so usually it's not too hard. It's a bit more difficult this time, because of what I know about the location of that final tournament, but I manage. Caledon works us very hard right up until the week before, and then leans off a bit so no one breaks anything because they're tired or stressed. Our routines are tightly choreographed; even the downtime between songs maximizes the use of time. We have ten minutes, total, and we must spend seven and a half of them actively cheering. The clock starts the moment I, as co-captain, touch the mats and it ends when Polly finally makes her exit. The penalties for going over or under are steep, but we have practiced enough that our precision is top-notch.

The bus ride to London is quiet. I can see everyone counting steps in their heads and mouthing the words to the music that will accompany our routine. We arrive three hours before our slot, and immediately engage in the very serious business of hair and makeup. I have no idea what the boys do, besides sit there and get more nervous, but this is when the girls finally wake up and start to act like the overly peppy girls I'm used to working with.

"Jenny, come and sit here," says Leftie, which is the nickname we're currently auditioning for the brown-haired Sarah. It's not going well.

Jenny comes and sits, and Sarah begins to weave the gold ribbon into her braids. Everyone has their hair done up as tightly as possible today, to minimize chances of disaster, which means fishtails and French braids for those of us with long hair, and about a million pins for blonde Sarah, whose chin-length hair defies even Polly's abilities as a hairdresser.

"It'll be fine," says Karen, when blonde Sarah raises her hand to poke at her head.

"I'm really sorry," she says. "I didn't think it would go like this when I cut it. I haven't had it short in forever. But I promise it grows quickly. I'll be fine by—"

She cuts herself off. No thinking about nationals. I will make her leave the room and spit if she says it, and she knows I will.

"Beach season," she says, even though that makes no sense at all.

"Hermione, you're up," says Polly, and I sit down while she plaits the ribbons into my hair. The boys are all dark haired, so they're the other half of our school colours. Black ribbon is

200

also much more expensive, so we're saving it for a special occasion. Polly barely tugs at all as she finishes my hair, and before I know it, I am crowd ready.

"Everybody up!" I say, and they all fall in for inspection. It sounds stupid, but it's much, much better to prevent wardrobe malfunctions in the locker room than on the floor. I go up and down the line, checking skirt lines and hair spray, until I get to the end. I spin for Polly, who grins and nods.

"All right, let's go find the boys," Polly says. She's so legitimately happy and excited that the fake cheer sounds more real than ever.

The boys all holler and catcall when they see us—in fairness I should note that the catcalling between Cameron and Alexis is mutual—and heads turn as we make our way towards them. It's part of our pregame ritual, and it's the part I like the best. You can't win without cheering on the floor, but you can feel like you have, and right now I feel like anything is possible.

"All right, huddle up," I say, and all eighteen of us crush together. "It's been a weird year, I know, but I wouldn't have wanted to go through what I went through with any other group of people."

This is totally not the pep talk I had planned on giving. Eyebrows are starting to rise. Leo is looking at the floor. I push on.

"You build me up, you guys," I say. "You build me up, and that's what cheerleading is all about. You make a person, a team, think that they can do anything because you believe in them. You believed in me, when I didn't believe in myself. And now I believe in you. I believe in us. We are the

Fighting Golden Bears, and we are going to win."

They whoop it up around me, and even Leo is smiling. I know that out in the audience, Caledon and Florry are waiting for us. My parents and a bunch of others made the drive down together, and they'll be cheering when we're announced. I invited Dr. Hutt, but he only said, "I think cheering on a cheerleader is a little existential for my tastes," and went back to running lines for *Macbeth*.

"Ladies and gentlemen!" I hear the announcer call, and I clear my head of everything except the routine. "From Palermo Heights Secondary School, the Fighting Golden Bears!"

We run out, all teeth and ribbons, and when the music starts, we are perfect. We do the whole routine, as we have done over and over again in practice, but this time it's real. This time, it counts. This time, when we finish, the crowd goes wild, and when the judges post the highest score of the day for our performance, the yelling gets even louder.

The bus ride home is anything but quiet, and when I get home, I am still elated. There's a party at Mallory's house, because her parents don't mind if eighteen kids are very loud in the barn. Caledon has threatened death if anyone drinks, but she didn't need to bother: Even Tig is afraid of Mallory's mother, and thanks her very nicely for the pop she kept on ice for us all afternoon. We don't stay too much past when it gets dark, largely because it's still a bit chilly for outdoor parties, and when Polly drives me home, I can't stop laughing and smiling and telling her how awesome we all are.

My parents are in the kitchen waiting for me, and as soon as

I come in the door, I know exactly why. For the first time since September, my parents sit me down for a serious, serious talk.

"It's not that we don't want you to go," Dad says right at the start. "It's not even that we think it's unsafe. It's just . . . you've made so much progress. You've made it this far by never looking back. Are you sure you want to start now?"

I wonder whether I'll be having this same conversation with Dr. Hutt on Wednesday. More likely, they've already called him themselves. I can't blame my parents for sitting back and letting the expert handle me. I've certainly never thought about it like that. I told my mother months ago that I needed her to be my mother, and that's still true. I suppose I'm just ready for them to be my parents on more topics again.

"I know you find it hard to explain," says Mom, "and that's fine. We don't have to understand. We just want you to say it out loud."

They have definitely talked to Dr. Hutt. I guess it makes sense.

"Okay," I say. "Here goes."

Dad smiles and stops shredding the serviette on the place mat in front of where he's sitting.

"The thing that has really kept me going through everything this year, and not just the fallout of my attack, but everything that happens to normal kids their last year of high school, is cheerleading," I say. "And I love it a lot, which you both know. So even though it means I'm out there in public, that's why I've kept up with cheerleading. It's something that I love."

Mum nods and sits back in her chair. She's not taking notes, but she does have excellent recall.

"You know in cheesy action movies how they're always all

'But if we do that, the terrorists win!'?" I ask.

"Yes," Dad says. "That's usually before the explosions start."

"Well, not to overstate, but that's kind of how I feel about going back to Manitouwabing for cheerleading," I say. "If I quit now, or back down just because of the location, I don't win. And I really, really want to win."

"That seems good," Mum says. "If you get blindsided by a reporter again, tell them that."

The newspaper article didn't give anything away, but I had told my parents about the ridiculous things the reporter had asked, just in case. Mum is even better at letter writing than I am.

"We're coming to watch, of course," Dad says. "Well, I am."

Mum had borrowed against this year's vacation to take time off for me last September. She could play the my-daughter-is-a-rape-victim card, but I'm glad that she won't, even if it does suck that she's going to miss me at nationals. I plan to kick some serious ass, after all.

"Well, that's why God invented cell-phone cameras," Mum says.

"I'm not sure God invented cell-phone cameras," I tell her.

"He probably had something to do with it," Mum says. "Did you eat at Mallory's? I'm guessing not. What do you want for dinner?"

Technically I'm in training, and therefore should be eating healthy. Still, I feel like living in the moment, though, which is why we end up having ice-cream sundaes for dinner.

"Never tell anyone I let you do this," Mum says.

"Don't worry so much, honey," Dad says. "She's already got an excellent therapist."

That's how I know we're all going to be okay.

PART 4

Now 'tis the spring, and weeds are shallow-rooted.

CHAPTER 28

THERE'S THE WHOLE MONTH OF May between provincials and nationals. I get accepted to each of the universities I've applied to, and so does Polly. On the first Saturday of the month, she comes over and we talk about our choices.

"Now we have to actually make a decision," she says. We're sitting on my bed with the promotional material from all six schools spread out around us. It's a bit daunting.

"At least you've applied to the same program at three different schools," I tell her.

"That was very clever of me," she allows.

Cheerleading does not qualify as a sport, even under Title IX in the US, so neither of us have an athletic scholarship anywhere south of the border. A lot of people assume that we would, largely because every now and then one of the cheerleaders from Palermo gets a scholarship for gymnastics, which does qualify. When Polly and I were in grade ten, one of the graduating students did just that, and went to the University of Florida, but most of us will go to Canadian schools on our own dime, or on whatever academic scholarships we can scrape together.

"Hamilton has really bad air quality," I tell her, tossing the McMaster brochure towards her feet.

"Yeah, but the campus is gorgeous," she says. "And it's a great teaching hospital. Besides, we live in the future! They'll probably build some kind of air bubble around it, and then it'll be totally fine."

"Uh-huh," I say. I'm shuffling my three brochures. I was an idiot, applying to three different programs like I did. I should have just picked one. "The Ancient Studies program at Carleton has a year abroad option with the University of Edinburgh."

"And they're throwing a tonne of money at you," Polly points out. "Who knew such a brain resided inside that tiny, blonde body?"

"Shut up," I say. "You're worse than Dr. Hutt. He claims that it's thanks to his tutoring."

"He's probably not too far off, you know," Polly says. "Between that and cheerleading, you've been hyperfocused this year."

"Please do not remind me," I say. "Don't let me pick a school just because it's far away."

"You were always going to go far away," Polly reminds me, which is true. "You were just also going to come back."

"If I went to Carleton, I'd only be able to come home for holidays," I say. "Not weekends."

"But you'd get to take the train," she says. "Plus you'd live in the capital city with the most widely fluctuating temperature."

"Seriously?" I ask.

"And only Ulaanbaatar gets colder," she adds.

"I'm not sure that's a selling point," I say.

"Hey, take it up with Queen Victoria," she says. "I think you'd like Ancient History more than straight-up Celtic Studies, don't you? Plus, you could always pick Celtic-type classes. If you go to Carleton, you'd get to see everything before you specialize."

"That's a good point," I say. I look hard at the Carleton letter. Polly's right. They are offering me a crap tonne of money, and the promise of an exchange to Scotland on top of everything else the department has going for it is hard to turn down. "No deep thoughts about Brock?"

"It was your safety school, and we both know it," she says, waving her hand dismissively.

"Hey, it's gotten better," I say.

"Whatever." She flops back on the pillows, and I lie back with her.

"So Carleton and McMaster," I say. "Points to us for not going to a place-name school."

"Indeed," she says. "And Hamilton and Ottawa are both on the train routes, so it won't be that bad."

"It'll never be the same again," I say, looking up at my

ceiling. I can feel Polly's breath on the side of my face, and turn to look at her.

"No," she whispers. "It won't. Nothing ever is. Would you want to do this forever?"

"Good lord, no," I say. "I think I've pretty much tapped out the capabilities of the Palermo Heights cafeteria. I'm ready for a dorm-style dining hall."

"You are completely ridiculous." She sighs. "Let's call the other girls and we can all do our residence applications together."

We live in the future, she said. I think I'm ready for that again.

Brenda's working, but Chelsea and Karen show up about five minutes after we get them on the phone. Mallory takes longer, since she's coming from out of town and also because it's haying weather. When she arrives at my room, she tells me that Dad wants to know if we're ordering pizza or if we plan to mount a raid on the kitchen later.

"And then he said something about Napoleon and Russia, but I wasn't really paying attention because I got a text from Clarence," Mallory says.

I go over to the door and yell as loudly as I can down the stairs: "Do your worst, Russia! We shall overcome!"

"What did Clarence want?" Karen asks. She unloads all her university stuff onto the floor because there's no room left on the bed.

"He got into business at Laurier, but also the double econ at Waterloo," Mallory says. "And somehow he thinks I'll be able to help."

Mallory is going to be a nurse, which she says is way less exciting than what any of us are doing, and I say it will probably mean that she gets a job much faster.

"People trust you, is all," Polly says. "Which is handy in a health-care provider."

"Thanks," she says, and winks.

"Polly and I have picked," I say. "I'm going to Carleton."

"And I'm going to Mac," Polly adds.

"Technically I'm going to Mac too," says Mallory. "But it's a combo thing with Conestoga, so I get to live in Kitchener."

"Lakehead!" Chelsea declares, and there is instant uproar.

"Why in all hells would you do that?" Karen asks, throwing a pillow at her. "You might as well go live on the moon."

There's a lot of joking about the relative lengths of blackfly season and the pervasive solemnity of the Canadian Shield, but I'm not really paying close attention. Thinking of the future like this is a lot like kissing Dion: It's something I'm glad to know I can do, but I'm not taking it too seriously at the moment.

"We'll never see any of us," Mallory says. "That's the whole point. It'll always be an occasion."

"That's enough," I say. "We're here to make sure no one lies too egregiously on their residence applications, not to talk about how miserable we're going to be for the month of September."

"Pass 'em in," Polly commands, and we all hand in our forms. Polly shuffles for a moment, and then hands them to me facedown. I close my eyes and pull one at random.

"Mallory!" I call out, and Polly hands me a pen. "Single or double?"

"Single," says Mallory at the exact same time everyone else yells, "Double!"

I take a closer look at the brochure. "You still get your own

211

bedroom. You just share the kitchen. Also it's much cheaper."

"Fine," says Mallory, "but if I need rescuing, I'm holding all of you accountable."

"Of course," Polly says.

We fill in the portions of the form that talk about how obsessively neat and quiet Mallory is, even though she's actually kind of messy. Karen says it's always better to lie about that sort of thing so you don't get stuck with a crazy person.

"If everyone lies, won't I get stuck with a crazy person anyway?" Mallory asks.

"Whatever, who's next?" I ask. I pass Mallory her completed form, and she checks it over.

We do Polly's form next, also forcing her into a double room though we don't exaggerate her cleanliness at all. Karen is living with her aunt, so we don't have to fill out forms for her at all, and we manage to make it through Chelsea's without making too many comments about her choice to live in Thunder Bay.

"And Hermione," Polly says, turning my form over and taking the pen back.

"Do your worst," I say.

Polly fills out the form, taking advice from everyone else, and it's not that different from how I would have done it. They would have let me take the single-room option if I'd pushed it, but the rooms at Carleton are actually decently sized, and I don't mind sharing. As an only child, I've never had to do it before, and I figure it's a good life skill to have.

Mostly, though, it feels good to be around people who know me so well.

Our futures decided, I get stamps from downstairs. Dad is cooking something that takes up most of the kitchen surfaces, so I decide we should order a pizza or two after all.

"I told you!" he yells as I go upstairs with the phone.

"You did!" I yell back. I shut the door with me on the inside, and take everyone's preferences for pizza toppings. You'd think by this point I'd know most of them by heart, but Karen is a bit of an experimentalist when it comes to pizza toppings, and there's usually some fairly complicated negotiations between her and Mallory, who prefers just cheese, before we make any phone calls.

At this point, most girls would probably break out the music and do each other's nails, but since we kind of do that professionally right now, we opt to pile on the bed and watch a movie instead. It's a tight squeeze, but we manage until Polly starts to get angry at the predictability of the plot and sits up to wave her arms around while yelling at fictional characters.

"Clarence is going to go to Laurier," Mallory reports at about the three-quarter mark. We've stopped so many times, for pizza, pop runs, and bathroom breaks, that I can barely remember what happened at the beginning of the film. It's winding towards the resolution now, though, one of those happy endings that only Hollywood can deliver. The bad guy will get caught and everyone will live happily ever after.

Mum has problems with movies now. She can't watch people get closure because it kills her. She barely even reads fiction anymore. She doesn't know I've noticed, which almost makes it worse because it means we can't talk about it. I want to tell her that it's okay, that I'm okay with not catching the bad guy. She's set on my living happily ever after, and in her mind, we need justice for that to happen, but I've already made my decision.

I'm going to go to Carleton, where I'll freeze to death in the winter and boil in the summer. I'll go on exchange to Scotland and find out what the hell haggis tastes like. I'll take the train and live eight hours away by car. I'll make new friends and, eventually, I'll stop being a cheerleader. I don't know what I'll be when that happens, but I'm not afraid of it. And I will do those things whether we catch the bad guy or not, because that had always been my plan. I thought I would stop on my own terms. I thought my speech at the campfire meant I was changing Palermo Heights tradition and rewriting the future. I thought so many things.

"Where's Leo going?" Chelsea says, and I'm even grateful that the reaction isn't much worse than some side-eye from Polly.

It won't be the traditional happily ever after, but I'm about done with small-town traditions. I've loved growing up here, and it will always be home, where I'm from, but it's finishing. The five of us will never get together like this again. Someday, I'll go whole weeks without seeing Polly. And that will be the life I've picked. You bet your ass I am going to be happy about it.

"Hey," says Polly, elbowing me gently while the others get up and stretch. "That is way too serious a face for the end of this movie."

The credits are rolling. I forget what happened at the big closing scene. But that's okay. I'll live.

CHAPTER 29

THE MOMENT I STEP OFF the school bus, I know I have made a mistake. I should have come up with my dad tomorrow morning, skipped the whole pre-competition hoopla, and avoided being at Camp Manitouwabing for one second longer than I needed to be. I didn't think it would be this bad. I didn't think I would smell the trees this much. It's a different season, after all—spring, where before it had been summer—and I thought that would be enough to make a difference. It's windy, so the lake is crashing against the rocks on the shore instead of the light touch it has later in the season. I close my eyes, and realize that I am closer to a panic attack than I have been in months.

"Hermione!" shouts Tig, and Polly takes me by the shoulders. She doesn't shake me, not quite, but it's enough to snap me out of it.

"Sorry," I say. "I wasn't expecting that to happen."

"Just stay focused," says Polly. She doesn't mean on winning the nationals.

Unlike when we were here for camp, the twelve of us Palermo girls end up in the same cabin. It's the one Polly had been in during the summer, and she gleefully points out all the places where bugs crawl in as we stake out a bunk bed on the opposite side. As co-captains, we should have taken the beds closest to the centre of the cabin, but we defer to Jenny and Alexis, who will probably be elected as our successors. It is going to be absolutely freezing at night, but we've all brought thick sleeping bags and flannel pajamas.

Polly pulls her swimsuit out of her suitcase and lays it on the bed. I am about to make a sarcastic comment about tanning when I notice that all the other girls are fishing their suits out too.

"What the heck is going on?" I ask.

It's Mallory who answers, not Polly, which is something of a surprise.

"We wanted to do something crazy as a team," she says. "The lake will be really cold, so it's just in and out, but, well, we didn't want you to get upset about it. We didn't want it to be a checklist or anything unless you want it to be."

"We've still put her on the spot, though," Jenny says. Ever since she accidentally spawned the rumour mill, she has been exceedingly careful about what she says to me.

"No," I say. "No, it's a great idea. Except I don't have my suit."

My bathing suit flies across the space between me and Polly, and hits me in the face. Everyone giggles.

"Thanks," I say. "The boys are outside, I assume?"

"Ready and waiting," says Astrid. She's grown again, and Polly had to redo the hem on her skirt on the bus because she'd forgotten. The stitches are a bit crooked, because every school bus ever made gives a bumpy ride, but it'll get by. Everyone has grown this year, whether we wanted to or not.

"Okay, then," I say, and before long there are a dozen girls in bathing suits and towels.

"Are we allowed to go swimming?" Mallory asked. "I didn't even think of that."

"I did," says Karen. "Caledon says we can go in the lake whenever we want, if we are stupid enough to do so."

"Let's do this before I change my mind," says Polly, and throws open the doors to the cabin.

The boys are waiting, T-shirts and swim trunks, and towels over their shoulders.

"It won't be that bad!" says Clarence. "I went in swimming at the cottage in May, and it was chilly, but fine."

"Your cottage has a hot tub," Mallory points out.

"We can huddle together for warmth," Tig says.

"I would just as soon kiss a Wookiee," Polly shoots back.

We all truck down to the dock. Quite a few other teams have already arrived, the better to miss cottage traffic, but there's no huge outcry as we marshal ourselves down by the lake.

"Some rules!" announces Tig. "Okay, there's really only two rules. Everyone jumps off the end of the dock. Once you're in, you stay in until the whole team has jumped. If for some reason you don't jump in and leave us all to drown, we'll come up with a creative way to get revenge."

"This is a stupid game," Polly whispers to me, but I am already long gone.

They had found me right over there, where that tree grows straight out over the lake before bending upwards to the sky. Those flat grey rocks and the one pink granite stone is where I lay, unconscious and half submerged in the lake. And now I am going to jump back in.

In the middle of the dock, Tig and Leo stand side by side with Eric right behind them. They appear to be debating order, and finally Eric just takes off at a run for the end. He yells when he jumps, short and sharp, and cut off well before he hits the water with a resounding splash. Tig and Leo are right behind him, and then both Sarahs and Astrid.

"How's the water?" Dion asks when they surface and stop splashing one another.

"Refreshing," says Eric. His teeth almost chatter, but not quite. "You should definitely join us as soon as possible."

One by one, we jump. The lake fills with splashing, shivering friends, and suddenly it's not scary anymore. It's just a lake. And I love to swim.

"Come on, Hermione!" yells Clarence. "It's freaking cold!"

I laugh, and I pretend the lake can hear me. I imagine that it knows that I am not afraid of it. We were both in unfortunate places. There's no reason why we should avoid each other. I take a deep breath, put my hands above my head, and dive. I cut cleanly through the water, which is shockingly cold, and surface next to Dion, who is treading water. I lie on my back, and the weak June sunset does what it can to provide heat. For a long moment, I float, feeling the water against me, and then Polly swims up behind me and drags me under.

I come up spluttering and she comes up laughing. Dion is laughing too, and I realize that I love to see him smile. Leo and Tig are treading water nearby, and for the first time in a while, Leo is smiling at me. Maybe he is starting to understand. I don't really care, though. I do not want to be anyone's model for becoming a better person.

"Can we get out now?" chatters Cameron. His face is slightly blue.

"I think that's a great idea," says Tig, and swims for the ladder.

A few of the girls try to walk out. It's possible, but uncomfortable in bare feet thanks to the encroaching plague of zebra mussels. Most of us just wait for our turn at the ladder. Since I was last in, I decide that in all fairness I should also be last out. I tread water near the ladder, but not so close that I get in people's way.

"You look happy," Dion says, breathing hard beside me. He can run and dance forever, but apparently treading water is harder for him. I'm not really surprised. Boys don't always float easily.

"I am," I say. "I wasn't sure I was going to be, but I am."

"That's good," he gasps. "What are you doing for the summer?"

"Working, probably," I say. "I don't know where yet. My parents were going to make me get a job last September, but then they didn't."

It's starting to feel more natural not to say. It's no longer avoidance or denial. It's just the natural flow of conversation.

"I'm working for Mallory's dad," he says. We push ourselves towards the ladder as the crowd thins. "Early mornings, but it means I don't work when it's superhot out, and I can spend time at the beach."

"Sounds good," I say. "Though personally I am hoping for an air-conditioned job at a shop."

"To each their own," he says. "But if you ever wanted to come and hang out with me in the afternoons, you're more than welcome."

I remember the kiss, and even though it can't possibly warm me against the cold June waters, it reminds me that I can be warm. That I liked to be warm.

"I'd like that," I say, and we both smile at each other like idiots.

"Come on, Hermione!" Polly says. "I really want a hot shower before dinner!"

Dion climbs the ladder, and I am right behind him.

"See you at dinner," he says, and heads off towards the boys' cabins.

"Did you let him kiss you again?" Polly asks, leaning close so that no one else can hear, but I don't care who overhears us.

"No," I say. "But I may have left the future open for such an opportunity."

"You are unbelievable," she says, flicking her towel at me.

"What, he won't be in grade eleven anymore." I dance out of range.

"Yeah, but you'll be a university girl who is going to Ottawa in the fall." Polly wraps the towel around herself. It is definitely too cold to take our time outside.

"I'll cross that bridge when I get to it," I say. "We can't all pick the same university as our significant others."

"That was a complete coincidence," Polly protests. I happen

to know for a fact that it was, but it still cracks me up.

"Whatever," I say, starting up the wooden steps. "When does St. Ignatius get here?"

"Amy texted me right before I lost cell service," she says. "They were just heading out."

"Ugh, they're going to spend three hours on the 400," I say.

"They'll also get to eat at McDonald's instead of the mess hall here," Polly points out. "Seems like an even trade."

"Speaking of," I say, and hold the cabin door open for her. "Mum packed me about an army's worth of food, and I bet you Mallory's dad did the same thing. We should totally have a picnic."

"And not tell Tig," Polly agrees.

When the St. Ignatius bus pulls in, just after the boys come out of the dining hall and see what we've been up to for dinner, Amy sees us from the window and she waves. Polly turns a little pink, but no one notices. Amy comes towards us, and when her face lights up you could almost believe it's because she's realized that we've saved her most of the potato salad.

CHAPTER 30

CALEDON WAKES US UP HERSELF at six thirty on Saturday morning. There is quite a bit of grumbling about that, because the list of performance order was posted last night at dinner, and Palermo Heights will be second to last to go. This means we won't be onstage until nearly two, if everything goes to schedule. And it never goes to schedule. St. Ignatius is first, at ten a.m. I wonder whether they're just getting up now, or whether their coach got them up even earlier.

"I don't want to hear it," Caledon says as Astrid rolls out of bed. "You all knew what you signed up for. I want to see you all at breakfast in fifteen minutes."

"I can't get dressed in fifteen minutes!" Blonde Sarah protests.

"Not dressed, dressed," Polly says, throwing on her warm-

222

ups and putting her hair back in a simple ponytail. "We've got all day for that."

"I still don't see why we're up so early," Alexis says.

"Neither do I," I tell her. "But when Caledon says jump, I don't even ask how high. Especially today."

Because of the day's schedule, breakfast is entirely a cold buffet. Jenny's parents own the Palermo grocery store, and they've donated a lot of moderately healthy snacks. This will keep us going through the afternoon. Our two o'clock time means we need to eat a light lunch. I do my best not to think about dinner. By then, we'll have either won or lost, and speculation is pointless.

"Hermione, pass the juice," Tig says. He's a coffee addict on days that aren't competition heavy, but he seems to be adapting well. Maybe he's taking caffeine pills. Those are still legal.

"Why are we awake?" Leo groans.

"Because we're going to be competing outside," Caledon says. "You've never done that before. This way, you can watch some of the early teams do their routines, learn the ground, and still have plenty of time to get ready."

"It's a great idea, Coach," Tig says. "I just wish you'd picked a day when I could have coffee."

"Stay strong, Andrew," Caledon says, sardonic to the end. "This is your last day as a Palermo Heights cheerleader. Make it a good one."

"We few, we happy few!" Tig says, clutching his chest as though he'd been shot with a crossbow.

"That's the spirit," says Caledon, as Florry passes her the milk.

By the time ten o'clock has rolled around, we are all braided and beribboned, and the guys have taken at least one nap. We sit together in the stands, close to the front and the corner so that we can leave as soon as St. Ignatius is done. More parents are turning up than I had predicted. They're all decked out in their school colours too, but I can tell by the fact that there are quite a few kids in the audience that Caledon is not the only coach who wanted her squad to have a look at the competition area.

The field has been rolled and flattened. Every rock painstakingly removed and every hillock pressed back into the ground. As we take our seats, the athletic coordinators are laying the mats, double-checking one another's work to ensure that all of the Velcro fastenings will hold and nothing will slip. The ground is dry—it wasn't a wet May—but it looks springy. It will probably be softer than the indoor courts we're used to. Since the field is outside, the regulations have been changed a bit to allow teams five minutes to prep on the field before their ten-minute competition clock starts. St. Ignatius, as the first team of the day, gets seven minutes. I'm not sure what Amy can do with the extra two minutes, but at this point, she's probably glad to have them.

"Conflicted?" I joke to Polly as the sound system buzzes to life behind us and the announcer begins to test the mics.

"Hell no," she says. "All's fair in love and war."

"Good," I say. "I'd hate to have you go soft on me now."

She grins, her teeth flashing, and St. Ignatius takes the field for their seven minutes. The announcer switches to music after introducing them, and before I realize what's happening, familiar music fills my ears.

It had been daylight, a sunny June morning, only a few seconds ago, but now it's the pre-dark of a late August summer night. We don't pick our warm-up music. They just play something popular and upbeat. Of course they'd pick this. The bass thrums in the ground beneath me, and the scent of pine fills the air. I can't hear the lake over the music, but I couldn't hear it then either. I didn't know until they told me. This is not something they told me. This is something I remember.

"Hermione!" Polly hisses right in my ear. "Dion, help me!"

They wrestle me down out of the bleachers and underneath where we are out of sight. I can still hear it, though, still smell it. And Dion is holding me up, beneath the knees and around my waist, and he is too close, too close.

"For the love of God, put her down," Polly says. "Just, just set her on the ground."

"Is her dad here yet?" Dion asks. He puts me down, but doesn't let go. I'm not sure I can stand. He is never going to kiss me again. Why the hell would anyone ever want to kiss me again? I can't even breathe properly.

"No," she says. "But I think we're okay."

"I don't think that's okay," Dion says, probably because he's supporting all my weight, but Polly's turned back to me and is ignoring him.

"Hermione, you are going to talk or I am going to slap you," she says.

I want to tell her that I'm okay. I want to be okay. I want Dion to stop looking at me like I am going to break in half. I want to dance in front of the crowd, to hear them yell for us, to fly and be caught by people I trust. But I can't do any of those things. Not anymore.

"Hermione, I am not kidding." Polly actually sounds scared. Great. I've broken her too. I have to breathe now. I have to breathe.

"I'm here," I say finally. Polly relaxes and somehow the sun is brighter. "Don't hit me."

"Where's your phone?" she asks. I really, really need the music to stop. Hearing it, remembering it, makes it hard to do anything else.

"In the cabin," I say. "It doesn't work, remember?"

"Come on," she says, hauling me to my feet. To my surprise, my knees hold and I don't collapse again. Dion's hands are stretched towards me, though. Just in case.

Polly pulls me towards the cabin and Dion follows, more confused than anything else.

"I have not," she says, strong and determined and beautiful, "put up with cheerleading for the last ten years of my life so that you could fall apart at the last minute. And neither have you."

It's true. Polly is a cheerleader because she wants to win. All year long, I've been apologizing for being a bad friend, and all year long Polly has been encouraging me to be selfish. We're not at odds, not really, she just wants to remind me why she let me talk her into this back when we were in grade five.

Polly barges into the cabin and leaves me standing awkwardly with Dion on the steps. He doesn't meet my eyes. I want to kiss him, but I don't want to kiss him, and everything is starting to spin again.

"You can go back, if you want," I say.

"No," he says. "I'm okay if you're okay."

"I really want to be okay," I say. It scares me, how much I want it.

"I know," he says.

Polly comes back with my phone, looking triumphant. "Funny story," she says. "The camp actually has decent cell reception. The trees block it down by the camper cabins, but the staff cabins are on a hill, and on a clear day, you actually get a bar or two."

"Really?" Dion says. I follow them up the hill towards the staff cabins.

"Who am I calling?" I ask.

"You're going to call Dr. Hutt," Polly says, not bothering to hide her rolling eyes. "And he is going to kick your butt from whatever golf course he is on, and then we are going back down there."

"He doesn't really get cheerleading," I tell her, dialling.

"He gets you. C'mon, Dion." She marches him down the hill as I hit send, and a few seconds later, Dr. Hutt's phone starts to ring.

"Hermione!" he says when he picks up. "I thought you had your big pep rally thing today."

"The nationals," I say. "And yes, I do."

"Then why the hell are you calling me?" he asks.

"I'm kind of having that breakdown you said I was going to have," I admit. It's a lot quieter than I was expecting. Now that I have said it, now that we are farther from the music, everything is coming back into focus, though the edges are frayed and I feel like I could unravel at any moment. "They're playing my song."

"Hermione Winters, I want you to listen to me very closely," he says. I don't really have other options, so I do. "There are

227

always going to be triggers. You will hear that song on the radio, or walk under a pine tree on a regular basis for the rest of your life. You will have a spotty memory of the night you were raped and perfectly clear memories of everything surrounding your abortion. There will be people you just don't trust and people you'd trust with your life. I can't say things like that to many of the patients I've treated, but I know I can say them to you. You are adaptable and brave. So adapt, and go win that silly dance competition so I don't have to counsel you through a developing inferiority complex."

"I don't mean to be insulting," I say. "But I still think you're the worst therapist ever."

"I know, dear. That's why it works."

I've never wondered why Dr. Hutt agreed to treat me. He had said he wanted one more case before he went into retirement, and I'd believed him, but I think it's more than that. He knew that there would be people like Officer Plummer and Leo McKenna, people who would come to define my attack as the watershed event in their own life. He knew that another psychiatrist would try to make their career on me, with papers and, maybe, a book deal if the court case was particularly juicy. Dr. Hutt wants none of that. He just wants to put me back together and go fishing.

And I want to win.

"Thank you," I say.

"You're welcome, Hermione." And then, with surprising sincerity he adds, "Good luck."

I hang up the phone without saying good-bye, and head down

towards Polly and Dion. It's been more than fifteen minutes. We've missed Amy's big performance. I can apologize for that now, and Polly won't tell me that it's okay. We're past that. We're putting it back together.

"I'm sorry I made you miss Amy," I say.

"I'll watch the video," she says, but I know she understands. "Let's get back down there. I want to watch the next group go, and then we should probably fix your hair."

"And mine," Dion adds. "I think it moved a whole centimetre when I picked you up."

"My heart bleeds," I tell him. Polly rolls her eyes, but she's smiling when she takes my hand.

When we get back to the bleachers, the cheering is not for us. But I pretend that it is.

CHAPTER 31

WE SPEND THE REST OF the morning sitting on the floor of the girls' cabin, pretending we're not about to die of nerves. Technically, Camp Manitouwabing, not to mention our coach, has a strict no-mixing policy when it comes to boy cabins and girl cabins, but since we're in competition mode and our schools signed that waiver, the policy is relaxed a little bit. Accordingly, we've dragged all the top bunk mattresses down onto the floor, and are holding what looks like the world's most bizarrely well-lit coed sleepover. We have five whole minutes to get used to the ground after they announce us, and now we have to decide how to use them.

"The left side looked fine," Tig says. He's sitting on my mattress and fiddling with the zipper on my sleeping bag. In front of him is a map of the field he's made out of pens and pencils, and what few of my bobby pins that are not poking me in the head. "But there's that slope on the right they can't have fixed."

"Our right or stage right?" asks Jenny. I'm glad she asked so I didn't have to. Polly and I did manage to see the second team, but they weren't very adventurous when it came to field use, and so we didn't learn all we wanted to. "I mean, the audience."

"Stage right," Tig says, gesturing to the pencils. "You could see everyone on that side had to brace themselves, and their tumblers almost lost it overcorrecting."

"So practice your tumbling pass first off," I say. Polly and I are sitting side by each, leaning up against the bed frame while Mallory and Karen look over our shoulders. Everyone is sitting very carefully, to avoid mussing uniforms or hair. It's a bit comical.

"And then the throws, I think," Polly says. "Not the straight up-and-down ones, but the one where everyone ends up in a different place than they started. Spotters, keep your eyes peeled."

"It can't be that dangerous," Alexis points out. She's fiddling with a ribbon and Cameron keeps moving her hand away from it so she doesn't mess it up. "Or they wouldn't be allowed to have it here. Plus, we all survived camp."

"Valid point," I say. "But humour me, okay?"

"I haven't dropped you yet," Tig says, and I don't say anything, because it's true.

There's a polite knock on the door, which means it can't be Caledon. I wonder whether it's my dad, somehow alerted to my quasi-breakdown, but when Karen opens the door, it's Amy who is standing there, still in her uniform, though her hair has been half taken out. It's all curly where the braids were and she looks younger than she usually does.

"Permission to come aboard?" she says. "I mean, I know technically I'm the enemy, but still."

Everyone looks at Polly, because she's usually the one who makes decisions like this, and it catches her off guard.

"Come on in, Amy," says Mallory, and I remember that she has been Clarence's best friend for a very long time, and is always good at noticing things anyway.

"Yeah," I say, "it's not like you can really damage us at this point."

I can see the remark hovering right on the tip of Tig's tongue as Amy crosses towards us. The team has respected Polly's privacy, which makes me very proud of them. But it's absolutely killing Tig right now. Polly looks at him with a calculating expression on her face, and then pulls Amy right down into her lap. Amy shrieks in surprise, and then starts to giggle.

"We missed your turn because of a thing," Polly says. Amy would have seen us leave the stands, but she also would have heard the music. She knows what it means. "How did it go?"

"Oh no," Amy says. "You're not getting any secret information out of me!"

"Jeez, Olivier," says Leo. "What good is having an inside source if you can't get her to give it up?"

The thing about Leo is that he's generally the nicer of him and Tig. His treatment of me, and Tig's, have been kind of a weird aberration, another hint that something had changed. So I know, absolutely, that he did not intend to say what he just said.

Tig starts to laugh so hard he has to lie down on the floor.

Leo turns a shade of pink I didn't think was humanly possible. Amy turns her face into Polly's shoulder, but I can tell she's shaking with laughter. Polly just looks completely shocked. She's probably spent all this time coming up with witty comebacks for Tig, only to be blindsided by the boy she's been giving the cold shoulder to for months.

"Leon McKenna!" says Brenda.

"No, no, you know what I meant!" he protests, but by then everyone has dissolved into hysterics. "I'm really sorry," he says to Amy. "I totally didn't mean . . . that."

"It's okay." Amy hiccoughs, still laughing. "I'm still not telling you anything, except that I think we did okay, and mostly I'm just glad it's over."

"The competition?" Polly asks.

"No," says Amy. "High school. My team isn't quite like yours."

That kills the laughter fairly effectively, but we don't all sink into maudlin contemplation. Nine of the eighteen of us will be going out on the floor for the last time today. It's the biggest exit by graduation we've had since I joined the team in grade nine. In many ways, it's the end of an era. More than anything, I want to go out on top.

An alarm beeps next to Polly's pillow, and she gets up to shut it off.

"That's one o'clock, guys," she announces. "Boys, out. We need to do our last-minute stuff, and then we'll meet you outside."

Amy follows the guys out, and we turn on one another, fixing ribbons and tucking away straying hairs. Last-minute makeup touch-ups are done. Jenny cracks her neck and Mallory yells at her. We're as ready as we're going to get. We join the boys outside and head over to the bleachers as a group.

Caledon is waiting for us, and we warm up doing our best to ignore the cheering and the music from the other teams. At quarter to two, she calls a halt and leaves us to stretch. She'll be watching with Florry and our parents from the stands, but she's brought us as far as she can. The rest is up to us.

"Bring it in," I say, and my team huddles around me.

Last year, we had done this and been full of hope. We had been good, but other teams were better. This year, I know we have it. We just have to find it and leave it on the floor. I take a deep breath. The pine is in the air, but it doesn't bother me anymore. The teams who have just come off the floor mingle around us. I can hear whispers, like wind in the trees.

"That's her," they say. "She's the one."

My team starts to break open, to find the source of the whispering and shut them down. This is the moment where I choose. It won't be the last time.

"Listen up," I say, and just like that, they are back with me. "This is our day. We didn't have to come across the country, or even that far across the province, because this is our day. We've practiced for this and trained and thought. Tig stopped drinking coffee and I'm pretty sure Jenny hasn't had ice cream since March Break. You've failed tests because of practice. You had late assignments. Each and every one of you chose to be here. You all chose to try out when the competition was stiff. You chose to give up ever sleeping in so we could practice in the mornings. You chose to limit your social life. You chose to make your teammates your friends as well. And you chose today.

"I've asked a lot of you all, on the floor and off, this year. And I'm going to ask one more thing." I'm almost whispering now, like the wind and trees, and my team is leaning in to hear me speak. "Choose to go out there with me, one more time. Choose to do your best. Choose to trust your team. Choose to win, and I know—*I know*—we can."

Tig starts the growl in the back of his throat. I've never mastered that, mine always sounds like a lion cub with an upset stomach, but I join in when the others do. It's the thing we save for nationals, our trump card to keep the other teams from Ontario guessing. We're the Fighting Golden Bears all the time, but on very special occasions, we dig deep.

"Ladies and gentlemen!" calls the announcer. "From Palermo, Ontario, please welcome the Fighting Golden Bears!"

We run out, all teeth and fury, and I watch the tumblers do their practice runs as the clock starts ticking. We do one of the cross-throws, just to see how it goes, and Tig reports that the ground is fine. We haven't ruined the effect, though. When we do it for real, there will be four of us in the air, and it will look much cooler. We have forty-five seconds to go, and Polly is marshalling everyone into their spots for when the clock runs out. Leo falls into place beside me, rolling his shoulders as nerves and adrenaline take their last run before instinct takes over.

"I'm sorry, Winters," he says, so that only I can hear. No one has called me that in months. I missed having him as a friend.

"Thank you," I tell him, and it's awful, because we are already wearing our fake plastic smiles. "Tell me again," I say. "After."

"I'll tell you as often as you want," Leo says. That's how I know he means it. He's not going to spend any more time waiting for an apology that's never going to come. He's grown as a person, and for the next five seconds, I don't care about the cause.

Then the music starts, and I know I'm going to fly.

CHAPTER 32

I DON'T SEE OFFICER PLUMMER in the crowd until after we're done. I never see the audience until after the music stops. Some of the girls and guys look for their parents for a discreet head nod (waving is forbidden by Caledon, on pain of many, many laps), but I never do. My focus is my best weapon. As a flier, a lot of my fate is in other people's hands, literally, so I do the best I can to keep myself steady in the hope that it will help the others keep me steady in the air.

So I do the routine. And it's perfect. We hit every landing, we point every toe. Tig gets more height on his tumbling pass than I've ever seen, and the crowd goes wild when we do the full-bore pass of the crossover basket tosses. At the beginning of the routine, my cheerleading smile is about fifty percent fake, but by the time Dion throws me up in the air and I sail past

237

Polly into Cameron and Clarence's waiting catch, it's all the real me. When the music stops, and we hold our formation for five perfect seconds afterwards, the audience cheers so loudly that a forest fire helicopter could have flown over my head and I wouldn't have heard it. Then we're off the mats, and into the kiss and cry, exactly when the clock hits zero.

Mallory is bouncing towards me, happier than I've ever seen her. She throws her arms around me, laughing and I think also crying, but it's so noisy I can't hear her properly. Her mouth lands near my ear, and I make out the repeated strains of "We did it! We did it!" before Polly and the other graduating students wade in, and we become a mass of arms and braids and giggles.

"Shut up, shut up!" says Leo, but he's not angry. He's only telling us that they're about to post our score.

Each team is scored out of sixty, with subcategories for choreography, synchronicity, creativity, technique, execution and style. Currently, the top spot is held by the first team out of British Columbia with a fifty-three. I think we were better, deserving of at least one perfect score, but the judges will have seen things I couldn't have seen, and they tend not to be so biased towards my own school as I am.

"Come on," whispers Tig. It's killing him that the posting is taking so long. The judges don't lack a sense of the dramatic either, and as the competition goes on, they tend to drag out the posting time.

"The score, ladies and gentlemen, for Palermo Heights Secondary School," announces the commentator. "Fifty-seven out of sixty! Rocketing them into first place."

The announcer goes on to break down where we lost our three points, but I can't hear him anymore. There are seventeen people screaming in my ear, and I'm screaming pretty loudly myself. That's when I finally look into the crowd, and see my dad jumping up and down, hugging Polly's mother, while Caledon and Florry holler and wave their hands around. Beside them is Officer Plummer, who is clapping sincerely, if looking a bit confused. A person's first cheer competition can be that way.

"Move out, guys," Polly says. We have to clear the kiss and cry so the next team can come in and do their setup.

I don't know how I end up on the edge of the group. Maybe I was trying to take the lead. Maybe I was walking a bit out of step. I don't remember. What I do remember is looking up as we started to pass by the team from North York, the third team from Ontario who got into the competition on a bye because Ontario was the host province. They were in Amy's pool, so we didn't face them at provincials. I don't know if they're better than us, but they couldn't beat St. Ignatius, so I'm not too worried. Additionally, their colours are red and black, and they all wear pants. Before right this minute, that was everything I knew about their school. As they walk by, I look up and, so quickly I'm not even sure it happens, I lock eyes with one of the boys.

I don't recognize him, not at all, but I recognize the expression on his face. It's the expression we wear when our parents say "Did you finish the milk and forget to put a new bag in the container?" It's the expression we wear when our teachers say "Did you finish the homework?" It's the expression that boy will be wearing when Officer Plummer says "Did you switch your DNA sample to avoid getting charged with rape and reckless endangerment?"

Or it will be, depending on what I choose to do next.

He's seen me dance. Before, at camp, and then right now. He has to know I am a real person, not an object. Maybe he thought he was being romantic, if bringing date-rape drugs to cheer camp could ever be considered romantic. Maybe he's just a jerk. In any case, he drugged me, took me away from my friends, raped me and left me in the lake. Now, the choice is mine. And he knows it. He has to go out there with a plastic smile and be enthusiastic about his high school mascot, and there might be a hammer waiting for him on the sidelines when he comes back. He won't know until it falls. Until I choose to make it fall.

I consider my options. I could scream bloody murder right now, but I have no proof. I could tell Polly, heck, I could tell *Mallory*, and she'd kill him for me. Or at least charge him en masse and see how he runs when pursued by a sleuth of bears. But that might lead to our disqualification. I want him to pay, of course, but I also really, really want to win.

His team has fully passed me now, and I have fallen to the rear of mine. At the front, Polly has missed me, and checks over her shoulder to see where I am. She says something to Karen and then falls back to stand beside me.

"What is it?" she asks. "Are you okay?"

"I'm fine," I tell her. Because I am. Right now, I have his entire world in my hands, and it feels very, very good.

"What are you doing?" she asks.

"I'm making a choice," I say. "How do you feel about vengeance?"

"There's some saying about digging two graves," Polly says.

"But if you can do it with minimal collateral damage, I'm down with it. Why?"

I look at her. She's all ribbons and short skirt right now, but I know what's underneath all that. When Polly tells people she's going to Mac because they have a good teaching hospital, most people assume she's going to be a doctor. They're wrong. Polly plans to be the first thing a newborn baby sees when it comes into the world, and she plans to help their mothers get them there. She would probably make a great doctor, but she is going to be one hell of a midwife instead. She looks completely harmless, except when her teeth are bared. In her heart, she's always been a bear.

"Stay calm," I say, and thread my arm through hers. I'm not strong enough to hold her back, not really, but I might restrain her a bit. "The tall one, with the brown hair. That's him."

Polly goes absolutely still. I have to double-check to make sure she's breathing. She doesn't look angry or vengeful, like I thought she would. Instead, like me, she looks contemplative.

"What are you going to do?" she asks.

"I haven't decided yet," I admit.

"Well, remember that Officer Plummer is here," she says. "If you wanted a professional or something."

"I don't have proof," I remind her. "This guy somehow evaded the DNA test. He really doesn't want to get caught. If I just throw an accusation at him, he might bounce past it."

We watch as the North York team finishes their huddle. I wonder whether they know. I like to think the girls would toss him out on his ass without second thought, and I hope like hell the boys would too, but maybe they didn't. Maybe when he'd told them about his summer camp conquest, they congratulated him. Maybe he'd left out the tiny detail where I didn't consent and they never put the pieces together. Maybe they're all just jerks.

"You have to choose something," Polly says.

"I know," I say. To be honest, I'm looking forward to it. He took away my ability to choose last time, left me only with black oblivion. Maybe now I'm just riding it out, enjoying the feeling while it lasts. Maybe I've let all the power go to my head. Dr. Hutt will probably be proud of me.

The announcer calls the team name, and the audience begins to cheer. They bounce out, a blur of red and black, and I see him throw a water bottle into the garbage can.

"Asshole," Polly says. "The recycling was right there!"

"Polly!" I say. "Go get a ziplock from Mallory. A big one."

"Why?" she says. Then she realizes why, and leaves like I've set her feet on fire.

I'm not sure of the legalities of this, the finer points. I mean, I know it works on *Law & Order*, but that's TV and also American. But he threw it out. It has his DNA on it, and he threw it out. I stand over the garbage can, my eyes locked on his bottle, as the music kicks up.

Polly comes back with the bag before the routine begins, and she has Officer Plummer with her.

"I love you," I say, because I really, really do.

"I know," says Polly, because it's true.

"You did really well, Hermione," Officer Plummer says. I'm not sure whether she's talking about the cheerleading or the part where the bottle might solve her crime. She snaps on a pair of gloves, even though she's in plainclothes right now, and Polly hands her the bag.

I watch as she pulls the bottle out, seals it carefully and labels the bag.

"I'll get his name off the rolls," Officer Plummer says. "We'll do an extraction and run the test as soon as possible."

"Thank you, Officer," I say, one more time. "You've been amazing."

She looks like she wants to tell me that I'm amazing, but mercifully she doesn't. Instead, she waves and heads for her car. Maybe she has finally figured out that I want to be amazing for something else.

"We'd better get going," Polly says. "Mallory had about a million questions, and they'll send out a search party if we aren't back soon."

"You just want Amy to kiss you in front of everyone when we win," I tell her.

"Shut up," she says, and takes my arm. "Today, everything is ours if we want it."

"Yes," I tell her. "It is." I'm not thinking about university or court trials or even cheerleading competitions. I am not worrying about the people who prayed for me or about being the "raped girl." I will not be a frozen example, a statued monument to there-but-by-the-grace-of-God. I have danced before and I will dance tomorrow. As I exit the field with Polly, I close my eyes and imagine a baby who never was and a little girl who was never anything else. They will be forgotten, for the most part.

And so will I.

EXEUNT.

ACKNOWLEDGMENTS

I WAS VERY ANGRY WHEN I sat down to write this book, and as a result it was kind of a mess when the first draft was finished. Thank you to my crit group—Emma, Laura, Faith, and RJ—who helped me through the first few rounds of editing, and to Colleen, who read it even though it doesn't have any magic or explosions. Thanks also to Christa, Jenn, and Sarah, who helped push the science as far as was reasonable, and who answered some pretty graphic questions in useful ways.

Josh Adams started going to the mat for this book in 2013. He gets stuff done. Also, he called me when I was 250 words from the end of the first draft and was very understanding when I said something like "I am really sorry, but I have to set the phone down and ignore you for a minute, because I literally have a paragraph and a half of this thing left to type." I think it might have been our third phone call. He hung up on me.

And finally, there are three people without whom this book would not exist. One of them is me (because I wrote it), one of them is a local politician (see above re: very angry), and the third is Andrew Karre (at one point, the working title was "Is It Teen Enough For You Now?" [spoilers: it was not]). Thank you for e-mailing ten thousand times about *Veronica Mars* and

Superburger and Cottage Traffic and Commencement, and for saying all those nice things about my first (published) kissing scene. Thank you even more for helping me push a book-shaped idea into a book-shaped book.

Exit, Pursued by a Bear was written at the Chapters Waterloo Starbucks in June of 2012, before I knew what I was doing, and edited two and a half years later, after I had (thankfully) learned a few things.

FURTHER UP AND FURTHER IN!

Author's Note

It was very important to me that Hermione have an excellent support system in this book. Her parents, friends, teachers, coach, minister, and community rally around her. She receives the medical care she requires. The police are gracious and helpful.

This is not standard procedure. Many rape victims are isolated, unable to ask for the help they need, much less receive it. A small blessing is that there are many organizations, in both Canada and the US, that offer support to those who might otherwise be left on their own.

In Canada, we have the Kids' Help Phone as a national phone number (1-800-668-6868), and website (http://www. kidshelpphone.ca/teens). In addition, each province has a website for the Attorney General, including links for Victim Services (Ontario's looks like this: http://services.findhelp.ca/ovss/).

The United States has the National Sexual Violence Resource Center (http://www.nsvrc.org/organizations), and also the Rape, Abuse, and Incest National Network, better known as RAINN (http://centers.rainn.org).

Finally, there is a good chance that somewhere in your life, there is a champion. She will be an older student. A teacher you have never had. The secretary. Someone else's mother. But that person will have a car and she will make time for you, and she won't judge or ask questions. Finding her might be hard; you might never have spoken to her before. If you're lucky, she'll find you. Trust her when she does, even if no one else has ever stood up for you. I gave Hermione a Polly, but I think Polly might be the least fictional person in the book.